Navaj

Pa.. .

Acceptance

C. S. Clifford

First published in Great Britain 2017

ISBN: 9 780993 195754

Printed and bound in the UK

A catalogue record of this book is available from the British Library

Edited by Clive Clarke

Cover by Anna E Howlett from Rosehart Studio

To Skyler Best Wishes C.S.Clifford

THE NAVAJO SERIES
By
C. S. CLIFFORD

Part 1. ACCEPTANCE
ISBN: 9 780993 195754

Part 2. QUEST
ISBN: 9 780993 195761

Part 3. DETOUR
ISBN: 9 780993 195785

Part 4. PENNANCE
ISBN: 9 719993 61143

For more C. S. Clifford Books visit www.csclifford.co.uk

For Catherine, Niruta and Pratigya.

Their efforts to become better writers inspired the first words of my own writing journey.

And for all those I taught over the years.

Chapter 1:
Niyol

The setting sun lowered herself gracefully through the evening sky of the Arizona desert. Even though her life-giving energy waned, her lengthening tendrils blessed the ground with crimson kisses, deepening the hues to flame-like fire.

Below the sun, mountains towered, in constant battle with the erosive forces of wind and sand. Long shadows stretched across the desert pan and allowed gentle relief from the still hot temperatures.

Thorn studded cacti and dried out shrubs littered the otherwise desolate scene, their drab and parched colours interrupting the predominate reds of this sun-baked landscape.

As the light faded, the early autumn temperature dropped, almost as quick as a stone thrown into a river plummets to its watery grave. Here it could descend from over forty degrees at noon to near freezing by the middle of the night.

An hour of light was all that remained of another day of solitude and reflection. Memories and regrets of times shared and unshared; words spoken and unspoken, drifted through his mind. Despite the passing of years, emotions ran deep and still felt raw.

Towards late summer each year, the old man made this same journey to honour his late wife by reflecting on their time together. It was more than that though, but he couldn't say what. Was it respect for his culture and his past? Probably not, most of his kind feared the dead. Was it then a sense of guilt, duty or even a penance? He'd asked these questions, and others, a thousand times and still could not decide with any certainty. Maybe all these reasons contributed.

What he understand was that he felt better, each time, for making this trip. In some unfathomable way, the journey revitalised his soul, and his spirits soared as he directed his thoughts towards those he'd left behind and would soon see again.

Niyol was a full-blooded Navajo Indian, now in his eighties. He laughed at the thought of his name, meaning Wind, so named because of his restless nature as a baby, and his refusal to remain still for any length of time, even at night during his sleep. As a young boy, he would never walk when he could run instead. His father once told him he should be called wind because of the speed he ran at!

Smiling at the passing memory, his long, thin face erupted into a maze of chiselled creases, mirroring the myriad of erosion lines marking the side of the mountains. He remembered his mother telling him he had wrinkles across his forehead when he was born. *If I was American, they could have named me Linus! he thought,* laughing aloud at his own joke as he rubbed fine specks of sand from his face. *I'm no longer like the wind; he thought, I no longer run; but my spirit is still restless. Maybe they knew my true nature.*

Niyol's dark-brown, hooded eyes scanned the surroundings for a place to rest for the night. Ahead, and just to his left, he spotted a recess in some rocks that offered shelter on three sides. Gently, he steered the old grey mare he was riding with just a little pressure from his knees.

He dismounted lightly; his six-foot frame still as lithe as a twenty-year-old and examined the area he'd chosen. He knew it was free from snakes; his horse would have shown alarm, but he checked anyway. Habits, forged years ago, had kept him alive this long, and he wasn't about to change now.

Satisfied, he turned back to the horse and unharnessed her from the litter she'd been dragging. He removed the well-worn riding blanket from her back, regarding it with affection. His mother had made it for him over sixty years ago to mark his desperate need to travel; black, white, blue and yellow, each representing a direction on the compass. The traditional design still revealed the many hours of industry and love his mother had devoted to it; and although the colours had faded, it was still usable, albeit a little threadbare in places. He owned several blankets, but this was the only one he ever used for riding.

Half an hour later he'd settled in for the night, with a small campfire burning and some stew bubbling gently in a pot to the side. The last of the setting sun had gone, and the darkness was complete in minutes. Niyol ate, listening to the silence of the desert. Two more days and he'd be home, but journeying over the mountains would be much harder. Each year he found the going more difficult, as part of the terrain was too dangerous to ride and forced him to travel many miles on foot.

His buckskin clothes were warm, but the temperature drop made him shiver, and after he'd finished eating, he reached for his riding blanket. Laying some wood on the fire, he noticed that his stockpile on the litter was getting low and vowed to collect more tomorrow when he left the desert sand behind.

He moved some wood closer to the fire for during the night before patting his mare as she nudged his shoulder for attention. Niyol removed the leather strap from his forehead, allowing his long, flowing, almost snow-white hair to fall around his face then, he lay back and closed his eyes.

Twice during the night, a sixth sense woke him to add wood to the fire, but each time he returned to his dreams in seconds.

When he awoke, he felt refreshed as the sun rose, shedding wisps of her golden light across the desert floor. Alert, he stood, shook the stiffness from his body and put the remains of his evening meal by the fire to warm. He drank from his water carrier and poured some into a container for his horse.

"Drink well Friend, for today we reach the mountains, where the journey becomes harder," he said, patting her with affection.

He ate his food and wiped out the pot with some dried shrub. Setting to work, he attached the litter to the mare and positioned his treasured blanket. Finally, he kicked sand over the dying embers of the fire, turned and mounted.

"Come, Friend," he said aloud to the horse, "Let us journey once more!"

Niyol had always believed you couldn't own a horse and never named him as some would. As far as he was concerned, horses or other animals stayed with a person because they chose to. He regarded her as a friend and so referred to her as Friend. She responded to his whistle, but only, he would say, because she wanted to.

Trust and familiarity cemented his relationship with the horse. He would feed, exercise and groom her in exchange for the occasional ride on a journey such as this, or for some help with anything life threw at him that was too physical for his ageing body. Theirs was a good relationship; affectionate, trusting and reliable, and one that had lasted the past seventeen cycles of the seasons.

Their travels continued that day in complete silence, apart from the constant rasping of the litter poles dragging through the sand, and by noon the terrain changed. The distant mountain range was getting closer, and the ground was becoming more uneven and rocky.

Niyol ate and drank on the move, eager to push on, but soon it was time for the mare to rest. He dismounted, removed the blanket and laid it on the litter. Feeding her on some dried grass from a sack, he then prepared water in a container for her. he lay down in the shade of an old cactus, closed his eyes and snoozed through the hottest part of the day.

When they started off again, the noise from the litter increased and formed a random musical pattern; bass notes interweaved their way into a more persistent rasping melody, as the litter hit small rocks and stones with increasing regularity. Soon there would be only the sound of the bass drum as the sand lost its battle for territory.

About a mile ahead, to the left of their present course, Niyol saw something reflecting on the uneven ground of a scree. They were miles away from the nearest road and nobody travelled this way; there was just no point. But there it was again; glinting, teasing, calling him.

High above the area an eagle soared in lazy circles, riding a thermal ascending from the ground. Suddenly, the warm desert breeze stiffened, as it is often does in these lands, and sent a contrasting shiver down Niyol's back.

The Navajo believes that an eagle flies high above the chaos of the world to meet with the creator, and Niyol wondered what chaos lay below it now. With a strange feeling of foreboding, he steered towards the flashing object and increased the mare's pace with pressure from his moccasin-covered feet.

Desert sand had now given way to scree at the base of an outcrop of rock as high as an old saguaro cactus. He dismounted, not wanting to risk injury to the mare, and asked her to wait as he clambered over the rocks.

The object continued to flash at him every few seconds, enticing him forwards, but the deeper he went on the scree, the larger the rocks became and the harder it was to climb. Some were just too big and forced him to traverse them to continue up the dangerous slope. Perspiration dripped from his craggy face as his effort increased. His body ached from the torment and screamed in protest from the exertion.

The meandering path disorientated him, and he stopped on top of a large rock to regain his bearings, no longer able to see the reflecting object. He peered around at Friend to check how far he'd travelled, grunting with satisfaction that he'd somehow maintained the correct direction; he was close!

Hearing its insistent call, he looked up and noticed the eagle flying lower now, in tighter circles, and forced himself to stop and catch his breath, what was the urgency; it was just a reflection of some discarded rubbish, wasn't it? Why then did he feel so tense? Why now the sickening feeling in the pit of his stomach?

In front of his lowered position, and at the base of a sizeable rock, were two even larger ones directly ahead and blocking his view. Knowing he had neither the strength nor agility to climb over them, he edged his way around. Here at the base, the rocks were smaller, stacked precariously, dangerous under foot. He craned his head, peering in front of him, and wiped his eyes on his buckskin sleeve. They stung in protest, as they do when you peel an onion, and his vision misted before clearing and coming to rest on a cloth-covered mound about ten yards in front.

At the hem of the cloth ran a series of metal eyelets which, even now, flashed a silent appeal in the midday sun.

Chapter 2:
The Discovery

Niyol clambered the last few yards, halting abruptly in shock as he gazed upon a human body, mostly concealed in the sack. in Bright, fresh blood, drying in the desert heat, covered the head. He knew that it hadn't been there for long and scanned the surrounding area.

Further ahead, where the rocks petered out and sand once more invaded, he discerned a set of tyre tracks heading toward Mason, a small desert fringe town. Niyol had visited there several times in the past, but apart from buying general supplies, there was no other reason to make the journey.

His attention snapped back to the body which lay face down inside the large hessian grain sack, presumably used to carry him. Smothered in bloody stains, but dry, the moisture had soaked into, and then evaporated from the coarse hessian.

With heart racing and body trembling, Niyol reached out an unsteady hand towards the blood-stained neck and searched for the carotid pulse. He felt sure he was too late, and the beat of life would be absent. So much blood!

Having seen the lifeless bodies of his parents and other members of his tribe at different times during his long life, and he'd always experienced mixed emotions. The sadness of a life passing, and the joy of knowing they were on their way to the spirit lands of the ancestors. But also, the worry that the spirit can take a few days to leave the earth and may cause mayhem before it ascends.

But time once spent in the western world had changed his perspective on death. He no longer feared it.

At first, he thought he'd only imagined the faint flutter and withdrew his hand. He wiped it on a rock and once more sought the pulse. Again, he felt it; there had been no mistake. Weak, almost non-existent, but enough to know that this person was still alive!

Niyol felt an overpowering sense of relief and a surge of adrenalin that launched him into action. Drawing his knife from its leather sheath, he cut through the rough hessian, until he'd uncovered the body. The amount of blood was frightening, but he knew that blood loss from a body spread and could appear worse than it was.

The body lay face down, stretched over two large rocks, sagging slightly in the middle over the gap between them. Niyol knew that he couldn't move it until he had examined it. He could make the injuries worse through careless actions.

Running his hands down the length of an arm, he felt for irregularities. No broken bones here. He grunted in satisfaction and repeated this action with the other arm and then both legs, with the same result. He felt the spine and back next, searching for the tell-tale signs of a broken bone and finding none.

His attention turned to the head. As he ran his fingers over the matted hair, he could feel several large pebble-sized lumps and his hopes flagged. The damage could be severe, even though the wounds had stopped bleeding.

Now he needed to turn the body over, to examine the front of the torso. He stood up from his crouched position looking for some smooth rocks to wedge underneath the middle of the body where it sagged. Finding some, he raised the mid-section enough to place them underneath. He straightened the arms and legs and carefully rolled the body towards him.

He sat up, shocked as he looked down upon the face of a young teenaged boy.

Who would do this to one so young? He wondered, battling feelings of outrage and horror.

Once more he returned to the search for injury. There were three raised protrusions about the chest, three broken ribs. As his hands moved upwards, he found that the same was true of the collarbone and the distorted shape of the nose suggested a breakage too.

Niyol had a decision to make. To move him was risky, especially on this rocky ground, as the movement might exacerbate his injuries. He could leave him and seek help; no, too time consuming, and the boy could die in his absence. Or he could just wait with him until he joined the ancestors in the spirit land; surely, it wouldn't be that long.

Looking upwards, he saw the eagle still circling high above; it cried out its haunting melody, and it was all the encouragement he needed.

"I hear you, great bird," Niyol called out.

There wasn't a choice at all; there was only one course of action to take, and he didn't hesitate.

Bending down, he lifted the boy, cradling him in his arms. He grunted at the effort and made a silent plea to his animal spirit for the skill and dexterity he would need to get off the scree. Step by painful step, he made his

14

way back down the slope; the journey taking much longer than before.

As he left the scree, perspiration ran down his face and his heart pounded from the effort; he lowered the boy to the ground. Retrieving his water carrier, he resisted the immediate urge to drink and instead trickled some into the boy's mouth. Once satisfied that he'd taken a little, he raised it to his own parched lips.

Bending back down, he checked the boy's pulse. For several seconds he held his breath, releasing it in a rush as he located its beat, deciding it was not weaker than before.

Walking to the mare, still standing in the shadow of a rocky outcrop, he stroked her neck in private thanks for her patience and loyalty before untying the litter. By the time he'd finished, a dishevelled pile of belongings now lay haphazard where he'd emptied it in haste, and he dragged the empty litter towards the boy. A natural stretcher for the forthcoming journey; the only comfort that Niyol could offer his patient.

He propped up the litter at a slight angle on some rocks at the edge of the scree and covered it with his sleeping blanket. Once again, he fetched his water carrier and trickled some into the boy's mouth. Then he fetched a small bowl, filled it with water and, using a soft leather cloth, set about cleaning up his patient.

As he worked, the true extent of the boy's injuries emerged. Contusions and lacerations covered his entire body. After cleaning the limbs and upper torso, he fetched a long strip of leather to use as a bandage to support the damaged ribs, securing it tightly around his chest. The protruding bones returned to a more normal position, and he said a silent prayer again, hoping he'd not punctured a lung. Next, he held his breath as he applied pressure to the collarbone and felt it move. Releasing it gradually, it seemed to have returned to its normal position.

Now Niyol noticed the sun creeping towards the horizon, and he lit a fire to the side of the litter before returning to his original task with fervour. Supporting the boy's neck on a mound of grass, taken from the horse's feed sack, he cleaned the matted blood from his face and hair. He studied the face, gasping in recognition and understanding at what had probably happened to him.

The boy's face showed that he was of mixed spirits. It had a roundish shape that held all the attributes of a Navajo Indian; full lips, hooded eyes and prominent brow but the skin colour was paler, a clear sign that one of his parents had been pale skinned. Niyol lifted an eyelid and saw that his eyes were blue, additional confirmation.

The savagery of the beating and the injuries inflicted on the boy were overwhelming. His eyes moistened with empathy, and his sudden surge of emotion surprised him. *Did you anger the spirits? he wondered.*

He snapped back into action. Using finger and thumb, he reset the nose with a minimum of force. Although swollen, it returned to its original shape.

The wounds on the back of the head were badly swollen and attempt stitching would be impossible, even if he had the equipment with him. He fetched his medicine bag and ground plants and roots to make a salve before applying it liberally to the wounds. Another strip of supple leather made for a bandage.

He checked the boy's pulse again. Was it his imagination, or did it appear to be a little stronger this time?

Leaving him, Niyol returned to the litter. There was a stiff breeze blowing across the desert and in the dimming light Niyol attached a blanket to long branches of firewood to form a windbreak. This he tied to the side of the litter, giving it protection from the wind.

Finished, he went back to the boy, muttered an apology and lifted him once more before laying him on the blanket. He wrapped and placed him on the litter. Trickling water into the boy's mouth, he stared at the battered face.

"Rest well and heal, my young friend," he whispered, then walked away to feed and water the mare.

Suddenly, the physical and emotional strain of the afternoon bore down on Niyol, and the overpowering need to close his eyes and rest became clear as he stifled an enormous yawn. He hadn't eaten since his morning meal but chewed on some dried meat rather than cook a meal.

Afterwards he lay back on his sleeping mat by the windbreak and closed his eyes. But sleep wouldn't come.

Chapter 3:
The Journey Home

Although he had closed his eyes and tried to relax, the anger he felt towards those who had abused the boy, increased. His thoughts turned to what might have happened.

There was still racial prejudice against Indians in this state; prejudice that had travelled the distance of time, since the fighting for their lands all those years ago. For those of mixed spirits it was worse; belonging to neither race, hatred often culminated in displays of brutality towards them, for no other reason than their being of mixed blood.

Whilst this may not have been the only reason, he would bet his favourite blanket that prejudice had played a part in it. Someone had kicked this boy and stamped upon him many times; the heel-shaped bruises on his body bore testament to that. Someone had beaten him almost to death, then dumped him in the middle of nowhere; his attackers never intended him for someone to find him. It was a hate crime, he was sure, and the attempt at taking life would have succeeded, had it not been for Niyol.

Just an hour later, frustrated at being unable to sleep, he rose and reached for the water carrier. After satiating his own thirst, he poured a few drops once again into the boy's mouth, worrying that so little was being taken. He stood, looking into his face, wondering if he would wake and hoping there was no other internal damage.

Feeling the night chill attack his lean, tired frame, Niyol returned to the fire, adding more wood. He sat enjoying its warmth, staring at the mesmerising flames and willing the torment in his head to leave him with a sense of peace.

He tried to concentrate on tomorrow's journey. Even though it was too soon to move the unconscious boy, he had little choice. His supplies were low and needed replenishing. Nature's abundant larder was just a day's travel ahead.

To drag the litter further, he would have to find an easier passage, his present course too rough and dangerous to carry a wounded boy on a litter. There was another route, he knew of a trail, but it would add time to the journey.

With his mind alert, Niyol sat out the duration of the night. Dripping water into the boy's mouth regularly, he knew that little was being consumed, but he had to keep trying. Then dawn stripped away the protective shroud of darkness.

As the first rays of sunlight spread across the vast land, he was already feeding Friend, talking to her in his native Athabaskan tongue as she ate. Then he backed her up to the litter, which required turning to face the opposite direction, and the mare.

He removed the simple leather reins from her head and used them to secure the boy's body to the litter. Next, he crawled underneath the front, where it rested on the rocks, and took the weight on his shoulders. Slowly, he stood upright and turned the litter until it was in line with the mare. With just a few steps he could rest it on the horizontal support rails and let Friend take the weight, while he secured it with the straps.

The litter was now resting at a greater angle than it had been, and Niyol checked that the boy hadn't slipped down, but the reins had served their purpose. Looking at his pile of belongings, he decided that the last of his wood would have to remain where it lay. The rest he loaded as carefully as possible, ensuring that nothing could slip and add further injury to the boy, before mounting the horse and setting off.

The trail headed towards the mountains and Niyol knew that he would reach them at noon. This time, however, the track he would take was several miles further on. It offered a gradual incline, and in places there were wide, smooth, sandy trails used by hikers and National Park Rangers, less fraught with danger.

They would pass a stream to refill the water bags, and he could gather a range of wild foods as they approached the tree line. Thinking of food made him feel hungry, and he reached into a leather pouch attached to his tunic, where he kept a supply of dried meat and chewed contentedly.

His attention turned to the boy's injuries. *I must check the head for infection. I must wash the bandage, for I have no other, he mused.*

An incursion of thoughts continued through the morning as they travelled, and it was past midday when they stopped, Niyol rebuking himself for not resting Friend earlier.

With a few miles left before the start of the climb, they'd made excellent progress. Still wanting to start the incline before nightfall, he needed to find the spring and a suitable shelter for the night. There was also the added security that beyond the tree line, the likelihood of his fire being noticed was less.

The temperature dropped as they started up the mountain; the path meandered through copses of shady conifers, and the wind funnelled down small ravines and passes. Soon they would stop to rest, but Niyol could see the tree line, an hour away, and relished the security that the forest would offer. Passing the spring, he filled his water carriers and, with the light fading, continued upwards towards the trees.

After another day had passed Niyol was travelling at a higher altitude now. The forest was thicker, and the trails were intermittent, and he navigated using his knowledge of the area, gleaned from past journeys and hunting forays. Tonight would be the last camp, for tomorrow he'd reach home.

As he washed himself in a small pool, he could see the physical toll he'd paid for the past four days of travel. His face, already gaunt with age, looked even thinner, the skin hanging limp from it.

Although his patient had still not moved or uttered a sound, his pulse was stronger now. The healing process had started, although Niyol wondered about the state of his patient's mind when he woke up; he'd seen serious head injuries like this before and the brain damage they caused, and he hoped that this boy would not suffer the same fate; he'd had been through enough already? He made a silent plea to the spirits.

Waking the next morning, he knew that it was later than usual. He did not berate himself for sleeping longer, for he knew how much he'd needed the rest. His mind felt clearer and the thought of only four or five hours of travel left made him smile for the first time in recent days, as he went about his duties.

This morning, chilly though it was, he stripped naked and bathed in the stream. His granddaughter could always smell him when he came back from travelling and threatened to wash him herself, if he didn't attend to it straight away. *That will not happen!* he thought, with a wide grin that transformed his chiselled face.

Naked, he hurried back to the litter to retrieve his spare set of buckskins. He dressed quickly in the pale morning sunlight, hoping his patient opened his eyes for the first time. Again, he grinned at the thought.

Attending to Friend and his patient, Niyol loaded the mare, mounted her and once more followed the sporadic trail, ever upwards and deeper into the forest.

Another hour passed, and the trail took a sharp turn, cutting across the incline on a more horizontal plane. The path followed this way for half a mile before descending on the opposite side of the mountain. There it petered out altogether. He ignored the turn and continued in the same direction, entering part of the forest he knew so well.

On this side of the mountain, the trees were not as thick, often concealing small glades, where pockets of the autumnal sun highlighted a diversity of green hues on the trees and shrubs. No other place in the world matched its beauty; in winter, the colours would disappear under a blanket of snow and only the evergreens would add colour to the desolate but beautiful scene. In late spring, when the snow had melted, the first of the seasonal colours would burst out, transforming the forest into a naturalist's paradise. This place was home, the place he wanted to live out his remaining years.

It was just past midday when he rounded the large, moss-covered rocks, incongruous against the mountain backdrop, and marking the boundary of the place he called home.

Chapter 4:
Home

As Niyol passed the rocks, the trees thinned out to reveal a clearing about twenty yards long and ten yards wide. On his right was a steep, almost vertical, drop off that was just high enough to clear the canopy of trees at its base. The view from here was breathtakingly beautiful; miles of tree-covered mountains, valleys and ravines that stretched as far as the eye could see.

To his left was a barren rock face that soared upwards for hundreds of feet with scattered boulders and rocks at its base. The dusty surface here was devoid of plant life, but human footprints covered the ground showing that despite the distance from civilisation, people were using this area regularly. Niyol dismounted, patting Friend as he did so.

"Is no-one here to greet an old man?" he bellowed.

From behind the rock pile, a young girl in her sixteenth year emerged at a run.

"I see you, Old Man!" she yelled back, laughing, as she launched herself at him from a distance, almost knocking him off balance.

They embraced fiercely.

"You have washed this time!" she said, a mischievous glint in her eye.

"There is no mountain I would not climb for you, Doli!" he replied, adopting a serious expression. "Let me see how you have grown."

"You are gone a cycle of the moon! It is too soon to show this," she answered.

But she stepped back to allow him to gaze at her fully; well versed in every little routine of her grandfather.

She was, in Niyol's opinion, the most beautiful of all the spirits' creations. Dark, suntanned skin accentuated her moon-shaped face. A slim, delicate nose and a gentle, soft, laughing mouth covering a perfect set of brilliant, white teeth, all contributed towards her natural beauty. She had restrained her long, black hair with a strip of rawhide at her forehead, in traditional Indian style, and wore a red flower above her right ear. She was the most beautiful girl Niyol had ever cast his eyes upon, more so than her mother, and even more so than her grandmother.

Doli had something extra, though, to mark her identity. Whilst her mother had been a full-blooded Navajo, her father had not, and the colour of her eyes represented him. They were of the deepest blue that Niyol had ever seen. Her nature matched her beauty; she was a capable person who saw only the good in her world and the people in it. Having infinite patience, she exuded the tranquillity of one at peace with both the world and herself.

"Hmm!" he exclaimed loudly. "You are more beautiful than before and taller I am thinking."

"Your great age confuses your memory, Old Man," she retorted, teasing him in return.

He grinned back at her, declining to respond to her jibe.

"What keeps your brother so busy that he cannot greet his grandfather?"

From behind the same rock pile, Doli's twin brother, Nayati, made his appearance.

"I see you, Old Man! No business keeps me from greeting you!" he said, with a smile almost as mesmerising as his sister's.

Nayati clasped Niyol's forearms with firm hands and then pulled him close for a bear hug.

"You get stronger each day, boy, and you fast become a man. But if your face gets much prettier, boys will prize you as well as girls," Niyol teased.

"You speak of this each time you return from your travels, Old Man, and I tell you there is no room in my life for these things!" he retorted.

Niyol grinned affectionately at the boy. He too was beautiful, sharing the same facial features, including the eyes, as his sister; but his body was firm; broad and muscular in contrast to the slim, lithe Doli. The buckskin clothing, he wore, contrasted the colour of his skin, and made him even more handsome for it.

"You made much noise travelling, I heard you far away!" Nayati rebuked his grandfather.

"It is true, Old Man! Never have we heard you make such noise on your return," Doli agreed.

"There is reason for this, my children, for my load was heavy," Niyol protested wearily. "Come!" And he led the way around Friend to the litter.

Niyol stood back slightly, allowing the twins space to see. Both gasped and stared at the sight on the litter. Finally, Nayati broke the silence.

"You have brought another here, this is not wise, Old Man? Is there not danger in this?"

Doli turned upon him and reprimanded him for his disrespectful comments, but Niyol intervened.

"There is no danger from one who sleeps so deep," he said.

"But when he wakes?" Nayati continued.

"He may not wake; his wounds are great. But he has powerful spirits that seek to keep him alive."

"Powerful spirits and you, Grandfather," Doli suggested. "Let us take him inside."

"Nayati, untie the litter. Grandfather, unload your things and make space near the fire."

Niyol smiled inwardly as he let Doli take charge, her maternal instinct as fierce as her mother's used to be. Quickly, he moved around the rocks that his grandchildren had appeared from and entered his home to carry out the task she'd set him.

The entrance to the cave was small, and he almost had to crawl to go inside. There was a second entrance to the right, above the level of the ground, of a similar size in height, but narrower, and used as a window.

Niyol had discovered this place over twelve years ago. Nothing had inhabited it, not even creatures; yet it had begged to become his home.

Once through the entrance, the roof of the cave ranged from ten to twelve feet in height and had a coarse and uneven surface. The primary area was a rough circle, about thirty-foot in diameter and was perfectly flat. There were six tunnel-like branches leading from it, all but one about four feet wide, continuing into the mountain for just a short distance. Niyol and his family used each for a separate purpose.

The sixth was wider than the rest and tapered towards the back. It had amazed him to find that there was water running across it; appearing from a small gap to the left, to disappear again through a small, low exit on the opposite side. The flow of water that passed through was roughly eighteen inches wide and about twelve deep. Niyol had never known it to dry up, even in the hottest summer months, or freeze in the harshest winter.

He had lived here for about three years, before bringing his grandchildren to stay with him. During the first year, he had built frames with doors for each of the rooms, out of wood he'd cut himself.

Each of them had a space or room of their own, if they wanted to use it, although at night they slept in the main living area. They used a fourth for storage and supplies, and the fifth for wood, cut ready for the fire. They used the water room as a washing area and for cold storage, as the temperature in there stayed a few degrees cooler than the rest of the cave.

The cave had another important feature. In the centre of the roof was a small hole that travelled through at an angle to the outside, allowing smoke from the fire to escape the cave, and ventilate naturally in the outside atmosphere.

Furnishings in the central area were minimal. There was a strong, but crudely made table, with two benches, pushed back against the wall between two room openings, and three open cupboards with shelves. Again the design was simple, but sturdy and functional. Doli had put cut flowers in a clay pot on the table. The sleeping mats, with blankets adorning them, lay on the floor around the rock-guarded hearth, added more colour and a softening touch.

Niyol had cut a rough timber frame for the window opening which they sealed, when required, with a trimmed sleeping mat and an extra thick, heavy blanket rolled up ready to keep out the cold air. Above the doorway they had rolled a second blanket in readiness to keep out the drafts. There were several moulded clay cups mounted on the rock face. These were full of oil with wicks that were lit when they required additional light.

Niyol looked around in appreciation at being home again but did not dwell on it for too long. Quickly, he gathered up the sleeping mats and blankets, pushing them from the hearth, just as Nayati and Doli dragged in the litter, carefully placing it down. With a glare at Niyol, Nayati stomped from the dwelling.

"Forgive him, Grandfather," said Doli.

"There is nothing to forgive, for he is right to fear for the safety of us all," Niyol replied.

"There is a better way to show it."

"Ah! Your brother is not you, Doli," he said, with a smile. "I can see and smell that the boy needs cleaning and fresh coverings for his wounds."

"I will do this, you can attend Friend, if it pleases you."

He knew it wasn't really a request. She took her duties seriously, so he left the cave to take care of his own needs.

By the time he came back, the boy was looking as if he'd had a bath.

"His wounds?" he asked Doli.

"Three broken ribs, but they are in place, collar bone too. You did well with these, Grandfather!"

Niyol stifled a need to laugh but didn't remind her it was he who had taught her about such medical matters.

"I fear for the head wounds; the cuts are deep and need stitching, but there is swelling. There is no infection, and I have used the healing salve. His bruises and cuts heal well and are full of colour. There are no sign of wounds inside him, and this is good."

Niyol took a deep breath for her, as she seldom said so much at one time. He told her he had given the boy only a little water.

"I will make broth tonight," she said, "it is full of good things for the body, if thin, I will give as water. It is little, I know, but is better than nothing."

"He is of mixed spirits, Grandfather," she added.

"This, I know."

She trickled water into the boy's mouth and Niyol sat, content to watch her, as he'd watched the women who had come before her, with the same sense of pride.

At last, she covered the battered body in a favourite blanket and sat back smiling at her grandfather.

"I shall want your story after food," she told him.

"You will hear it if you are quiet," he chided.

Doli smiled at him.

"You are tired," she said perceptively, "you must rest."

"There will be time enough tonight," he replied.

"An eagle flies above us? It is so since your return."

He looked at her in surprise but did not respond.

Chapter 5:
The Family

Nayati returned just before the evening meal was ready. Doli joked that his stomach could tell the time, more so than the position of the sun in the sky. But Nayati was in no mood for jokes or idle talk. He sat in his usual position with a far-away look in his eyes.

During the meal, Niyol told them about the trip. He spent a long time leading up to finding the boy, deliberately keeping his audience waiting, and building the anticipation with the skill of a true storyteller.

Suddenly Nayati could wait no more; "Forgive the interruption, Grandfather, but tell us of the boy with mixed spirits," he demanded, almost spitting out the words in frustration.

Niyol looked at him impassively. "Your sister has asked the story of me also. It would be wrong to leave out the details."

Nayati glared at Doli, who stifled a smile, none too successfully.

"Build up the fire, clear these things and I will continue; the sun is low and there is coldness in the air."

Infuriated, Nayati fetched more wood. Doli took the food bowls to the water room to clean, but not before giving her grandfather a raised eyebrow and smile. Niyol stared at her without a shred of expression on his face, then lifted the palms of his hands upwards. His feigned innocence made her smile broaden, but she said nothing.

Ten minutes later they sat around the fire, listening to the rest of the story. Niyol's recollection for detail was excellent, and he continued for some time before he completed the tale.

"It is not right to bring the boy here. You bring risk to us," Nayati stated.

"There is no certainty of this. It is not known where his path may lead. If I left him to die, would it not be true that I were as bad as those that did this to him?" Niyol asked.

Doli replied quickly, before her brother spoke without thinking. "Your choice was wise, Old Man. It was right to do this. I am glad you found him, and not one with less duty towards another life."

Nayati changed tack and asked, "It would seem that the eagle is his animal spirit, it has stayed since the boy came?"

Niyol paused before answering. "It is the way of an animal spirit to reveal itself to a person in a chosen moment, it is rare to reveal itself to others first. Only time will show the truth of this."

Doli walked outside. The night sky, already devoid of sunlight, was darkening fast. She looked up, making out the shape of the eagle, high above. When she returned, Niyol did not glance her way.

"It is still there, Granddaughter?" he asked.

"As you knew it would be, Old Man!" she replied, smiling. "You must sleep tonight, Grandfather. I will care for our patient through the night, you can help tomorrow. The demands on you have been many, you need rest."

Niyol nodded his response and turned to Nayati.

"Autumn will pass soon. Before the snows of winter come, we must gather the supplies we need. You are becoming a man, Nayati; I am becoming older and slower. I ask you to take on this duty. Will you do this for me, Grandson?"

Nayati was quick to recognise the honour of responsibility and replied.

"There is none who could do better than you. This you have shown through the years. I will do as you ask of me, if you guide me still."

"For as long as I have breath," Niyol replied, and laid his hand on Nayati's forearm.

Nayati let it rest there a moment, then placed his own hand on top of Niyol's.

They sat deep in the silence of their home and the turmoil of their thoughts, before Niyol announced his intention to sleep. Each collected their sleeping mat and blankets and laid them in their usual positions. Nayati built up the fire and lay down.

At first light he woke to find that his sister's position had moved. During the night, she'd moved her mat alongside the boy. His first thought was that the boy might have awoken, but a glance towards the prone figure showed he hadn't moved.

Doli saw his glance and told him that she had moved rather than disturb either of them in the night, while attending to the boy.

Nayati said nothing and hid his feelings of displeasure. He felt something else too; he wanted his sister to have nothing to do with the boy. The feeling was strong, unexpected, and it irritated him. He shifted the focus.

"I have work that will not wait, cutting wood, and will be gone until sunset," he told her.

Knowing instinctively, that he wanted to be alone, she replied. "You will need food; there is broth from last night. Take it to replace the strength you use today; I will cook you a warrior's meal tonight!"

"You are a good sister," he said, expanding his chest and standing tall. "I will go now."

Doli grinned to herself at the size of her brother's ego!

As he left the cave, Niyol was looking up. Nayati's eyes followed the direction of his Grandfathers gaze and saw the eagle.

"Still it is there, Grandfather. It must be the boy's animal spirit!"

"Of this it is too soon to say, but the eagle keeps him within its sight."

Nayati did not respond, but questioned the logic of what Niyol said, for the eagle couldn't see inside the cave. Instead, he stated his intentions for the day. Niyol insisted that he tell him exactly where he was going and explain how he would cover the scars of his work behind him. Nayati explained that he would cut down the tree at the lowest point, that he would spread the chippings over a wide area, and how he would cover the remaining trunk, so that nobody would know a tree once stood there.

"You are wise to take such care, Grandson. Even I might not find the place where you have taken this tree from the forest," Niyol told him, pride clear in his voice.

"I am only as wise as he who taught me. All I know I have learned from you, Old Man," Nayati replied affectionately, leaving to fetch Friend and the litter.

Soon after he had gone, Doli emerged from the cave and sat down beside Niyol.

"The day is beautiful, Grandfather," she observed. "The spirits are smiling!"

"They smile each time they gaze upon you, Bluebird."

Doli blushed at the translated use of her name; he used it rarely and only in moments of great contentment.

"How is he who sleeps?" he enquired.

"There is little change, but he heals, and I believe that his body would get stronger if more food was inside of him," she replied. "Grandfather, were you not worried bringing him here to our home?"

"It should be so, but I am content with this. Do not ask why, for I have not the answer. But the eagle is a sign, of this I am sure. A boy should die from these injuries, but he did not. He is strong and the spirits are not ready to take him. It is my thinking he has purpose, but what? This I do not know. All will be shown in time; it is the way of things."

"I hope you are right, Grandfather, I respect the knowledge you have gained over the great many years you have lived!" she replied cheekily.

"There are times, child, when I would not allow such disrespect; but believe me when I say that I am not too old to do this..." he said, almost wearily.

His slow, gentle manner of speech had lulled her into a false sense of security, as, with the speed of a rattlesnake; he twisted suddenly, digging his fingers and thumbs into the area just below her ribs. She giggled and laughed, until he stopped, then rested her head on his arm with a sigh.

"It is good to have you back, Old Man," she murmured, "I miss you when you are away."

"And I you," he whispered. "Now let us eat!"

The following morning, Niyol spoke to his grandchildren.

"Soon I will go to the trading market for the things we cannot find in the forest. It is my thought that you will come with me, Nayati; your sister will care for the boy."

"You will leave her here alone, with him?" Nayati asked, surprised at such a suggestion.

"We travel four days. The boy is no threat; when he wakes, he will be weak," Niyol continued.

Doli interrupted, "It is as Grandfather says; I can take care of us. Go Brother, it will be good for you. You will share your stories, when you return. It is settled! Go together, and soon; before the first snows," she said, with a finality that did not need further discussion.

They left the following day, allowing enough time for Nayati to finish filling the wood supply and for Doli to sort her wares for trade.

She excavated the collection of baskets she had woven and stored away. Nayati had helped her stain some with natural dyes from the forest, and often suggested geometric patterns for her to use, for decoration. He never helped her though; traditionally, this was a woman's task to perform.

Niyol gathered some carvings of animals and birds he'd made during the previous winter. Some, he had carved in intricate detail, while others held only a hint.

Nayati brought out one or two of his own he'd made under Niyol's tutelage. They were almost as good as his grandfather's, and he remembered with pride, the praise Niyol had given him on their completion. There was one of an eagle that Niyol had particularly admired.

"Leave the eagle!" he instructed, taking it and instead placing it by the boy's head. "He needs help from the spirits. Let it be a token."

At first, Nayati had resented the fact that his labour, so diligently undertaken, was given away, but his sister reminded him that the spirits would take pleasure from such a generous gesture.

Doli then retrieved the many skins from the animals they'd hunted, since the previous market. Each prepared to give a soft, durable finish.

Slowly, they loaded their wares onto the litter.

A day later, as Doli had suggested, the two Indians waved a last farewell to her and disappeared into the forest.

Chapter 6:
The Trade Market

"I worry that Doli is alone, Grandfather," Nayati stated, after they had travelled only a hundred yards.

"I see that, Nayati. You have looked behind many times since we left the camp. You are right to worry, for you are her brother, but I tell you this..." he paused, deep in thought, before continuing. "Doli is older than her sixteen years; she uses thought, sense and instinct. In her, this is stronger than in others I have known. If tested, her actions will be right."

"What if...?" Nayati started, but Niyol cut him off.

"We can talk about, what if's, for the length of this trip, Grandson, but I will say this, and then the matter will rest.

"There is a time, when a man or woman must journey alone; this is the way of life. It is my thinking that she is ready for this and will have much to tell when we return."

Nayati did not pursue the conversation, instead he honoured the silence of his grandfather as they journeyed, trying to heed the old man's words; but it wasn't easy.

They took it in turns to ride and walk for about an hour at a time, trying not to add to Friend's burden, and at noon they stopped to feed and water her. Nayati untied the litter and lifted it effortlessly. Niyol noticed and admired the lean, youthful body that was broadening at the shoulders. *He is growing into a fine man, he thought fondly.*

"Tomorrow Grandson, I will explain the customs for a good trade. It is so that we do not draw attention. We must go in, trade and leave quickly. It is wise to trade with few people."

Nayati responded with words that would please his grandfather. "I will listen well, Old Man, so that things will be as you say."

After an hour, they loaded Friend and started off again.

Part of the route they took was the same as Niyol's trip into the desert. Once out of the tree line, they would head west towards the town of Mason, before turning north two miles before the town. They would camp in places he knew, isolated spots that reduced the chances of meeting others. If luck held, they would have no contact with anybody until they were almost there.

Years of experience taught Niyol which traders to deal with. Exchanging goods for goods, he could usually get anything he wanted without the exchange of money. He was grateful there were others, who wished to trade in this manner, these seasonal events thrived on it. The trade market stayed open for several weeks with variable opening times to suit the demand for wares.

People came to revisit old friends and acquaintances and celebrate their culture, as much as for the trade. Most evenings saw traditional music, dancing and storytelling alongside more western style entertainment.

It had been many years since Niyol had taken an active role in the proceedings, although there were still some who remembered his skill as a storyteller and requested his involvement. He always declined, citing his advancing years and failing memory as the cause, unwilling to tell the true reason.

At camp that evening, Niyol fetched a package from the litter and brought it back to the fireside. Nayati watched, his curiosity piqued, but remained silent. The old man unwrapped two pairs of denim jeans and two checked shirts; he passed one of each to his grandson.

"You must wear this tomorrow, for if we wear buckskins, we will attract attention. The people in traditional costume do this for selling to tourists, or if they dance and sing in the way of the Dineh at night."

Nayati looked at the clothes, frowned, but said nothing.

"We will wear these until we return to this camp, in two days," he said solemnly.

Nayati had not seen, or worn, clothing like this for nearly ten years, and it never occurred to him that he might have to wear them once more.

"You are not at one with this," the old man offered. "It is hard for me also, to betray the clothes more suited to our lifestyle, but there is need for two days only."

Nayati nodded and again refrained from comment.

"We should sleep now," Niyol said, then added, "Do you still worry about your sister?"

Nayati considered his answer thoughtfully.

"I listened to your words with great attention, Old Man, and I hear the wisdom in them, but it is strange to be without her. I cannot remember a time when she was not near my side."

"This is new for you, Grandson, but this will happen more as you grow in years," Niyol said, in his usual serious tone.

Nayati did not reply.

The next morning, when Niyol awoke, his Grandson was already up and loading the litter on to Friend. He was wearing the strange clothes.

"Who is this stranger in my camp?" asked Niyol, with mock surprise.

"The wearing of these things; is not made easy by your humour, Old Man," Nayati answered, with distaste.

Niyol rose saying no more, then garbed himself in the same attire. When Nayati turned, he too laughed at the sight of the old man in his new outfit.

"See us both," he said. "It is good that Doli is not here; for she would speak of it forever!" Niyol laughed with him.

"Let us eat and take to the trail, Grandson," the old man said. "I feel we will laugh more, before this trip is over."

They ate a quick meal, broke camp and set off.

"We leave the mountains behind soon, the adventure will begin," Niyol told him, imagining the boy's excitement building as they drew close to their destination.

Nayati had already pictured the scene of the trading market, such was the strength of Niyol's storytelling abilities, and his anticipation was increasing at the thought of new experiences. Since moving to the mountains with his grandfather, almost ten years before, the old Navajo had isolated him from the world and everyone outside the family. The thought of meeting new people brought a range of feelings, from apprehension to excitement. He also knew that, apart from Niyol, his only living relatives were distant cousins and of Western origins. They would not have supported Niyol's past actions.

Once down from the mountain track, they changed direction towards Mason, twenty miles distant. The trail became flat and sandy as they fringed the desert, and their speed increased with the easier terrain. The deepening hues of red and orange, as the sun descended, were such a contrast to the greens and greys of their home. Nayati commented on it and Niyol told him that the colours would deepen even more at sunset.

He told the boy that they would camp a few miles outside Mason, after they'd headed north. It was far enough away from any roads and should leave them undisturbed. The following morning, they would leave early to reach the trading place before it got too busy.

By dusk, they reached the campsite Niyol had mentioned, one he'd used several times before. Nayati decided not to make a fire to avoid the notice of others; he felt his excitement building in anticipation of new experiences the next day. Niyol had been right about the colours of the desert, it reminded him of the mesmerising effect of flames.

At first it surprised Niyol that Nayati wanted to sleep early that night but guessed correctly at the reason. He simply wanted the night to pass quickly.

The break of dawn found both travellers ready for the remaining two hours of the journey.

"The world has been without you Grandson for many cycles of the seasons. You will meet people, who do not follow the traditional ways; some do not show respect in our way, or value all life as the Navajo," Niyol started. "Do not judge them, for the world is full of many peoples, with different ways and customs. This does not make them bad, it makes them different."

41

Nayati nodded. "I hear you Old Man, and I remember many stories you have told us of this. It might be hard at first, but I learn quickly. It will be as you say."

"You speak the truth, Nayati, and it is good for a man to understand his strengths and weaknesses. We are almost there; enjoy and learn from this."

Niyol ended the conversation, and as they rounded a bend in the trail, the trading market stood before them.

Spread over a vast stretch of barren land, people came from miles around for supplies of every kind. Filled with the sound of engines revving and horns blaring, the traders arrived at the site, leaving the scent of gasoline fumes hanging in the air.

Blaring music, coming from vehicle radios, interrupted the sounds of people meeting, greeting, laughing and calling out.

A variety of trucks, open-sided vans and lorries were each loaded to the brim with merchandise. Some trucks had their tailgates open, with furs and blankets overflowing onto tables or spread on the ground.

Tepees scattered around the site marked the spots for traditional Navajo clothing, jewellery and trinkets along with baskets and containers of every shape and size.

Open-sided tents sold western boots, smelling of leather, and clothing hanging from custom-made racks.

Stalls with awnings for protection from the sun revealed a rainbow of fresh-smelling vegetables and fragrant fruits. In one area, a hotdog stand with the surrounding air redolent of frying onions and sausage, stood next to a tepee offering traditional Navajo food.

Nayati stared at the scene, trying to take in the apparent chaos it all at once. His Grandfather noticed this and smiled inwardly. Dismounting Friend, he walked alongside his grandson. Normally, he'd go straight to the traders he'd used before, to speed up the process of trade, before leaving quietly. This time however, he deliberately journeyed around the entire site, enabling his grandson to absorb the sights.

"The noise offends my ears, Grandfather, and the smells, my nose!" Nayati offered, wrinkling his nose at the assault to his senses.

"This is the way, when many are together in one place," Niyol replied.

They passed a small gathering of people at the side of a flat-bed truck, watching the unloading of the vehicle. Nayati halted and stared at a part of the crowd. Niyol paused, his eyes following his grandson's.

"Is it the goods, or the girls who sell them, that take your interest?" he asked.

Nayati flushed slightly. "The clothes they wear are not right for this cool air," he said, still staring at two girls in light cotton dresses. "Do they try to catch a cold?"

The Old Man grinned at this.

"Maybe they try to catch a mate, Grandson, and maybe they try to catch you!"

Nayati flushed again. "It would seem that I have much to learn, Old Man," he said, grinning back at his grandfather.

They headed towards a trader that Niyol had bartered with before, several seasons ago, and started negotiations for some tools. Nayati watched with interest but remained silent.

As the morning moved towards midday, they'd exchanged most of what they'd brought for other things. Niyol head towards a tepee and an Indian dressed in traditional costume. He was selling buckskin clothing and moccasins, but also had sacks of corn and wheat seed for spring planting. Niyol bartered, offering some of Doli's baskets for seed. The Indian had placed a single sack of seed in front of him, for six of the baskets. Niyol looked ready to accept the trade when Nayati suddenly spoke up.

"Forgive the interruption, Grandfather, but..." he said, in a quiet voice.

Niyol immediately lifted his hand to silence him, but Nayati continued. "Forgive the interruption, Grandfather, but I cannot allow you to trade these baskets for one sack of seed. There are many baskets for trade here today, but none match my sister's work. It would dishonour her, to trade these for so little."

For once Niyol thought of nothing contrary to say, before the Indian tradesman interjected. To Niyol, he said.

"It is becoming rare that the young follow the traditional ways, showing respect to their elders. It is rarer that one will talk about honouring his sister. This, I admire." He turned back to Nayati. "It is true what you say, these baskets are of a high quality and, in the traditional way, I will not dishonour your sister by trading unfairly. Take two sacks, boy, and keep to the ways of our ancestors!"

Nayati and Niyol nodded in agreement and left.

After leaving, Niyol led Nayati away to a quieter area, out of earshot from others,

"Nayati, what you did was right and fair, and you honour your sister; but I fear we draw attention to ourselves. That man will now remember us."

Nayati thought for a while before replying.

"I hear what you say, Grandfather, but would that man remember us less, if he had kept to the first trade and gained so much from us?"

Niyol looked at his grandson with pride and respect.

"You may be right Grandson; you please me by the wisdom you show."

He made a vow to trade more realistically next time; Nayati had been right!

They'd finished most of their trading by early evening and were preparing to leave, when Nayati stated that he wished to find something for Doli, as she was not here with them. Niyol agreed that this would be a good thing to do and Nayati reminded him of the traditional necklaces that they had seen at one of the Indian tepees.

"I would trade for this alone, Grandfather," he stated respectfully, "I will practice what I learn from you today."

Niyol nodded and watched his grandson as he set off towards a group of young people that included the girls from earlier that day. He mused knowingly and smiled. *The dance between man and woman continues.*

Chapter 7:
Encounters

Nayati head towards the two young girls behind the makeshift counter. Confidently, he strode towards them, although he felt anything but. He told himself that he'd traded well earlier, with his sister's baskets, but this was different. That trade had been with a full-blooded Navajo Indian who respected and adhered to the ways of the people.

There was a small group at the stall who hadn't been there earlier, and as he headed towards it, he noticed they were all female, dressed in the clothing of the Western world. He observed that at least two were native Indians despite their clothing, one on either side of the counter.

Even as he approached, he could smell them, sickly, sweet scents of flowery perfume wafted up his nostrils. His nose twitched at the overpowering nature of the smell. Their voices, a cacophony, a flock of birds migrating south.

Western music blared from a rectangular box to the side of the table, adorned with a dark cloth to show off the trinkets for sale. The base thumped a rhythm, making the sand shake, before travelling through his body and into his head. How can they survive this attack on the senses Nayati wondered?

Still, he strode forward until hesitating a few yards from the counter where one of the two girls behind it spotted him. She nodded wide-eyed to the other members of the group who also turned. Seeing him, they separated, allowing room for him to reach the table. All had stopped talking and stared at him open-mouthed.

Six in total and the four not standing behind the table closed back inwards surrounding him and leaving him with little more than inches to move. Their proximity trapped Nayati, and he looked into the eyes of those who cramped him. The directness of his stare had an entrancing effect on the girls who each inched away, unable to match and hold the intensity of the gaze.

He turned his attention to the two behind the counter.

"I am Nayati of the Navajo," he said, sending a frown towards the radio that continued to blare out sounds he did not like.

The Indian girl reached over and turned down the volume knob until the sounds ceased.

Nayati repeated his greeting and the girls behind him giggled in amusement.

"I'm Laura, and this is my friend Haloke," the other said.

Nayati turned to face the gigglers behind him and gave them a look that showed their behaviour displeased him. They looked down and edged away from the stall calling out something unpleasant when they'd moved enough distance away. Nayati couldn't make out what they said but knew it was detrimental.

"Take no notice," Haloke said, but the extra colour spreading across her face showed that she'd heard and understood the comments.

"They are of no concern Haloke for it is a trade that I seek here," Nayati said, smiling to ease her discomfort.

"It's rare to meet a young man of the people who acts and speaks in the traditional ways Nayati."

"I have lived in this manner since the spirits blessed my presence on this earth."

"I don't mean to be rude, but you talk strangely," Laura stated.

"It is as you say. I live in a place far from others, there is little need of talking."

"Oh, so you live on a ranch. I had a friend who lived on a ranch and she didn't talk much either," Laura interrupted.

Nayati smiled making no attempt to correct the girl's inaccurate guess.

"You speak in the western way Haloke," Nayati changed the subject.

"Born and Bred in Muirfield. My parents left the traditional life on the reservation when they couldn't get work. It was hard for them to make the change, but they did it and now they make a comfortable living teaching about the Navajo ways in schools across the state, showing traditional arts and crafts. They taught me about the old ways though."

Laura didn't seem to like her friend dominating the conversation and cut her off.

"So, what brings you to our stall then Nayati?"

"I seek a gift, a gift for my sister."

"Is it for a special occasion, a birthday or something?" she asked, moving in front of Haloke and forcing her to move backwards.

"My sister could not visit the market, there is an injury."

Laura took the story on with no further detail from Nayati.

"Oh, the poor thing, did she fall off her horse or something? How nice to have a brother that cares enough to buy something nice for you? I bet my brother wouldn't do that for me."

"Do you have a brother or sister Haloke?" Nayati asked, trying to bring her back into the conversation and wanting to talk to someone who listened.

"I'm an only child but if I had a brother, I would like it to be someone as thoughtful as you." Haloke blushed.

"There are many things here Haloke, my sister would like these. Of this I am sure. Which of these do you like?"

Laura, realising that she no longer held Nayati's attention withdrew and rearranged some clothing hanging from a rack to the side of the table. A look of annoyance spread across her face and a bitter taste curled her tongue.

I'm better looking, with a better figure than Haloke; what could Nayati want with her instead? Boys are rubbish at finding the right girlfriend. She bent forward towards him affording him a glimpse at her ample cleavage to get his attention but Nayati's focus was elsewhere. She disappeared into the van parked nearby muttering under her breath.

"I like this range of necklaces, my mother made those, and I made these. This one is one of my favourites," she said holding it up.

"It is good, you would place it on your neck so I can see how it is?"

Haloke held it up, and the coloured beads and stones complimented the shade of her skin.

"Well, what do you think of it?"

"It sits in agreement with your neck Haloke, as it would on my sisters. I am thinking that this is the gift I choose."

"I'm glad that you like it; it's one I made myself."

"There is skill and patience in this. There are more?"

"One similar, but not the same."

She reached out and lifted it from the table. Nayati could saw the differences between the two but they were fairly insignificant.

"I would like it if they belonged now to me," Nayati signalled his intent.

Haloke named her price.

"I have no dollars, but I would trade with you if you agree."

"What are you offering Nayati, you've nothing with you?"

"It is small but take many hours to make," Nayati said and reached into a leather pouch that hung at his waist.

He emptied the contents onto the table for her. She gave a little gasp of delight at the sight of several carved animals and birds and examined them closer. She picked up a horse, modelled on Friend, noticing the fine detail of the work and then at those of squirrels and rabbits with similar detail.

"Did you make these?" she asked.

"During the long winter months."

"They are beautiful, I love them."

"Will you trade necklaces for carvings?"

"Yes!"

"What is your offer?"

"One carving for one necklace."

"I am in agreement."

They exchanged the items and Nayati packed away the rest of his carvings.

"Nayati why do you want two necklaces the same, girls prefer different ones?"

"This one is for my sister," Nayati said, choosing the second of his purchases.

"And the other?"

"This is your favourite. You should not part with it. Wear it around your neck so all will see how good it is."

Nayati handed it to her and waited while she put it on.

"Your help is good Haloke, this will please my sister."

Haloke smiled. "Will you visit my stall again Nayati?"

"I travel home soon but may return at the spring market. We might trade again."

"I would like that. There is music and dance here tonight, my parents and I will be here. Would you like to come with us?"

"I will ask my grandfather who I travel with and it may be so."

Nayati smiled, turned and made his way back to Niyol.

"We have traded enough," said Niyol. "It is time to leave. Everything we need for winter and early spring is here."

It was true. Nayati looked at the litter behind Friend. It was full, as it had been at the start of the journey. They had seed, hay, dried foods and oil to supplement their own stockpiles and new tools to work their many gardens. There were modern implements amongst the goods; a sewing kit, a new axe, and Nayati's worn-out hunting knife was replaced. There was also coffee, for which Niyol had a fondness. A few new cooking utensils, to replace worn-out or broken ones, lay wrapped against a small sack of salt. The list was endless, but the trading had gone well.

"Grandfather, I hear music and dancing are to take place when the sun goes down. This I would like to see."

"From who did you hear this?" Niyol asked, a smile on his face.

"It is from Haloke the girl who helped with Doli's gift."

"There is no time for such matters. We must return home for we would be away too long."

He noticed a brief flicker of disappointment pass over the boy's face.

"It would be unwise to draw attention by staying longer."

Nayati, knowing that his grandfather had made a wise decision, accepted his words without question at first, but, as he took hold of Friend's reins and led her from the marketplace, he decided to broach the subject later. Niyol followed behind.

"Old Man, I continue to feel strange in these clothes. The stitching rubs at my legs and my shoulders cannot move," Nayati said as they journeyed. "Let us travel later, so we can dress in the manner we are at one with."

"I too am strange in these clothes; we shall make it so," he replied, and they journeyed into the early evening.

Nayati changed before they made camp and Niyol followed his example. The old man questioned his grandson about the trading and what he had learned. The responses Nayati gave him showed he'd been attentive and learned. He complimented him by saying how proud he was of the way he was growing up; of the wisdom he had displayed and the loyalty he had shown for the traditional customs of his people. Nayati glowed at the praise and then brought up the issue that had been playing on his mind since they left the market.

Chapter 8:
Entertainment

"There is a matter I would discuss with you Grandfather."

Niyol looked across, seeing the troubled look that Nayati expressed.

"Speak of your thoughts Grandson, for to do other will make longer the problem in your mind."

"It is my thoughts that I will return to the market, the entertainment Haloke spoke about will be good."

"Why is it you think this after the warning I gave?"

"I wish to see what I have not before."

"Is it because Haloke will be there?"

"It is good that she will be, but it is not the reason."

"What is the reason?"

"There is music and dance in the Navajo tradition. There is also story-telling of the Navajo ways."

"These are good things, but more that is not good."

"What is there that is not good?"

"There is also music and dance that is from the Western people and many take part in smoking and drinking."

"Why is this a problem?"

"The smoking is not of tobacco; it can dull the way a man thinks, and he can act in strange ways."

"Too much drinking can make men fight each other. It is bad for they involve others who do not choose to fight. Many get hurt, some break bones. The risk is great."

"I hear what you say Old Man and I have listened well to your warnings, but it is my thoughts to go."

"I cannot allow this Nayati. There is a risk still that someone will recognise you."

"This is little chance of this Grandfather for I have changed much over the years. The choice to go is mine to make. I am old enough to make this and I go."

"If this is so, I must go with you."

"It is so Grandfather, I will go alone as I do into the forest to cut wood."

Niyol was astounded. Never had Nayati gone against him after being given such strong warnings. He paused from saying anything further, knowing that it would not sway Nayati's decision to go. Niyol, at sixteen, had been doing what he wanted for two years, such was his inquisitive nature.

Maybe it is time to let him loose a little, and Doli. They are both capable and sensible individuals with a strong sense of right and wrong. Maybe I should involve them in decision matters from now on and let them find their way. It is better than risking conflict with them, as we depend on each other so much for our existence, he mused.

"It will be as you say Nayati." Niyol stated, as if he had decided for him.

Nayati recognised the trust Niyol had placed in him.

"I will watch for the bad things you say about and stay far from them."

"You are wise. You will wear the Western clothes?"

"I will go in the clothes that I wear in the mountains. Many will be in the clothes of their people and I will look like many others, I am thinking."

Niyol realised he was right and nodded.

"Will you take Friend?"

"Friend has worked hard for us and will stay and rest. I will run and walk the distance."

"It is good that you consider Friend in this way."

"It will be late when I return, I will be silent so as not to wake you."

Niyol realised that Nayati was telling him not to wait up for him and smiled. He dipped his hand into his pocket.

"Take these coins Nayati for you have nothing to trade for food and drink. There is much on offer to try."

Nayati accepted them with a grateful smile, turned and walked back to the market. His walk soon increased to a run settling into a long striding gait that ate up the miles between Niyol and the marketplace. It was dark by now and Nayati allowed the orange glow in the night sky above the market to guide him the last couple of miles. Sounds of music and singing reached him well before he arrived, and a tingling of excitement surged through him.

Dressed in a costume he did not recognise, the first group of people that he came to were adorning two-piece, bright coloured suits. Jackets seemed too long to be right; their hair looked wet, combed back, but higher in the front. Many had a curl hanging on their foreheads. The women too wore bright colours. Short skirts that stuck out from their bodies in a semi rigid manner. They wore something on their feet, inside their shoes and extending up to their ankles.

Nayati thought they all looked strange and wondered what tribe they belonged, even though they were Western not Navajo. He noticed that none of them were playing music; the sounds they listened to came from a small box shaped item that sat close to the group, like the one he had seen at Haloke's stall. What type of dancing would go with music like that, he couldn't imagine?

Moving further into the market, it surprised him that some stalls had remained open for trading, despite the late time. He approached Haloke's stall and spotted her amongst the same group that had been their earlier. By chance she looked toward his direction and he raised his hand. She moved away from them and headed toward him.

"I didn't think you would come," she said, lowering her head, suddenly coy.

"I am thinking I might like the things you told of,"

"Perhaps, I could be your guide if you like."

"My time here will be better for your company."

"We could start by getting something to eat first, the dancing will start by the time we finish."

She slipped an arm through his and led him away.

"I have travelled far and am in need of food."

"What sort of food do you want?"

"I would like it if you make the choosing Haloke."

"There is a Chinese man that cooks amazing oriental food that I like."

"I have not heard of this tribe."

"Chinese is from China, an enormous country in Asia. He cooks Chinese food. Rice with many things in it."

Haloke said, trying not to show surprise at his ignorance of China.

"Where did you say you come from?" she asked.

"I did not say, but it is a land far from here."

The Chinese man was barefooted and seemed to dance around his large campfire as he moved from one large frying pan to another. The smells that reached Nayati's nose were delicious and doubled his hunger.

Haloke pointed to a dish of rice and meat and held up two fingers. The little man placed two portions on paper plates and offered it to them. Haloke took some coins and gave them to the man.

"I have coins for this Haloke," Nayati stated.

"I wanted to pay for this as you gave me that necklace earlier, you did something nice for me and I wanted to do something nice for you."

Nayati nodded his acceptance.

They sat down at one of the little tables by the man's stall and ate their food. Nayati commented on how good it was and Haloke smiled at having made the right choice.

Their discussion turned to dancing and Nayati told her that he wanted to see traditional Navajo celebrations. She took his arm again and led him to another area where dancing was already taking place.

Men and women in full Navajo attire, stepped and bounced their way in a circular direction all to the musical beating of a dozen drums. Those dancing, were singing in the native Athabaskan language and Nayati couldn't help wishing he was amongst the dancers. As if reading his thoughts, Haloke asked if he would like to join in.

"This dance is new to me. I would like to know it so I might teach my sister."

"It is not too hard, just copy what the person next to you does until you no longer need to." Haloke grinned and led him toward the dancers.

They spent an hour dancing and singing, and it was only Haloke's insistence that forced Nayati to leave it.

After buying drinks Haloke led Nayati around the rest of the festivities stopping at different dancing to witness the style and compare it to what he'd just done.

They were almost back at Haloke's stall when a group of youngsters ahead spotted them and moved in front of their position. Nayati recognised the girls from the stall earlier in the day. Haloke recognised them too, knew they were drunk and that they would be trouble.

"Turn around Nayati, let's go down there," she said pointing towards a Navajo trader's stall. There were two men there, sharpening knives on stones.

"I am thinking that we are going to your stall."

"That group in front of us are drunk Nayati, there will be trouble, I know them."

Nayati remembered the warnings of his grandfather and turned as she had suggested.

They almost reached the Navajo knife sharpeners, when the group they tried to avoid cut them off.

"Hello Navajo boy. You are Navajo aren't you, sort of? Now that I look closer you might be American. No, I've got it, you're neither, your half and half aren't you. You're one of those low-down stinking half-breeds, aren't you?" The girl that had called out something rude earlier that day spoke out with venom.

Nayati made to speak but Haloke spoke up first.

"You've had too much to drink Clarissa and as usual you speak before you think."

"You keep some strange company Navajo girl, why mess around with a half-breed?"

"I choose the company I want, and it doesn't matter where they come from."

"Me and my friends don't like half breeds, you can't trust a half-breed, most of them are thieves."

Nayati got his chance to speak but couldn't hide the confusion in his mind as he searched for reasons behind the threat in front of him.

"These things you say about me have no truth. You do not know me so do not judge me."

"Knowing one half-breed is knowing all half-breeds."

The boy who spoke out moved forward and stopped right in front of Nayati, so close that it compelled the Navajo to step back. Three more youths moved forward and took up positions to the side and behind him.

"Hit him Jimmy, show him what we think of and what we do to half breeds," Clarissa goaded.

Jimmy clenched his fist and raised his arm but a shout from behind stopped him.

The trader who had been sharpening his knives had moved forward brandishing one at least twelve inches long.

"You are looking to show off your skills with a fist. Brave of you, four against one. Isn't it time you fought like men? Why not take me on with a blade? Come on, I'll give you each a knife and you can take me on, four against one."

The four drunk boys stood still and didn't make a sound, each watching the blade in the man's hand meandering from side to side.

"What no takers. Come on, boys. I'll tell you what, let me show you what a knife can do if held right."

60

He moved forward and inserted himself between Nayati and Jimmy forcing Nayati to take another step backwards. The man waved the blade close to Jimmy's face. Jimmy's eyes bulged with fright and beads of sweat formed on his forehead.

The boy behind Nayati and the two at his sides slipped away back to the safety of the group. Jimmy's eyes followed the weaving blade.

"If you get good with the blade, you can do this."

The blade danced across the front of the boy's shirt so fast that he shook. Feeling the slightest touch, he looked down. There had been six buttons on his shirt, but it was now open, and the buttons had fallen to the ground. A wet patch appeared down the front of the boy's trousers and the man taunted him more.

"Having a little trouble with the bladder, are we? Look everyone, this brave young lad has wet himself. He'd better go home to mummy and get himself cleaned up."

With that Jimmy ran off as fast as he could, away from his friends, away from everybody else.

"You all right Haloke, I don't think they will bother you again."

The other group moved away.

"I'm fine thank you Uncle Fred thanks to you."

"How about your friend here?"

"I am well. The skill with the knives has taken many years to learn I am thinking," Nayati spoke for himself.

"Been practising all my life. It is rare that somebody else apart from me that appreciates it though. Take care of yourself lad because there are lots like him around here, ignorant of the fact that we're all humans no matter where we come from. Nayati nodded."

Haloke took his arm once more, and they walked away towards her stall.

"How can this man be your uncle?"

"Not my blood uncle but as good as. When I was younger and my parents had to go somewhere, he watched over me. He's a good man, a caring man and I love him like a real uncle."

"It is good to have a man such as this in your life"

They reached the stall and Nayati announced that he had to leave.

"Will you return Nayati, I would like it if you came to visit me?"

"I live far from here, but I will return to trade after the snow has cleaned the earth. It would please me to visit you then."

Haloke moved closer and wrapped her arms around him in a hug. It took Nayati by surprise and a moment passed before he hugged her back. He experienced a longing deep inside that he didn't understand and then a sudden sadness at their imminent parting, but he hid it from her as their embrace ended.

"Look after yourself Nayati."

Nayati turned and started the long journey back to camp making a mental note to question his Grandfather about why the colour of skin was so important to people. And why those of mixed spirits were so hated.

Chapter 9:
Confusion

It was well past midnight by the time Nayati reached the campsite. As promised, he entered as a mountain cat on the hunt and Niyol didn't stir as the boy lay down and pulled his blanket up to his chin.

He lay for a moment staring up at the multitude of sparkling stars wondering if the spirit world reached as far as them before deciding they must. Replaying the events from the evening in his mind, he knew he'd made the right decision to go. But his thoughts turned to the ugliness he experienced.

Why was it that these people, who didn't even know him, showed hatred towards him? Why were the people of mixed spirits such an issue? He'd not been disrespectful towards any of them; he'd been polite and patient. That boy wanted to hurt him. Why? What would he have done had they attacked him?

The questions and lack of answers worried him more and more and he couldn't shake the feeling that he might have been in trouble had it not been for the intervention of Uncle Fred. At home Nayati was always confident in everything he did but he realised, that in the moments before Uncle Fred faced up, he had not known what to do and was vulnerable. It hadn't felt good then, and it didn't now.

The cracking of a piece of wood snapped his troubled thoughts. It was a little distant but there was no mistake. Nayati suspected a mountain lion and stood up. He walked two paces forward and picked up his bow. Then knelt, placed his hand on his grandfather's shoulder and shook it.

"Wake Old Man, for there is a great cat close by and he has reason to visit us I am thinking," Nayati whispered.

"Have you seen the great cat?" Niyol whispered back.

"I have not, but it trod on a stick and it broke."

"A mountain lion would not make such a mistake. It is likely that this is a human hunter."

"There should be no other but us here."

"You are right and yet there is. It is my thinking they followed you from the market."

"Why would..." Nayati started, before his voice ceased.

"You have knowledge of who it could be?"

"I am thinking this."

Niyol retrieved his own bow and then indicated for Nayati to get behind a large rock. He did not hide himself though as Nayati walked away.

Both strained their ears listening for the tell-tale signs of somebody approaching their camp. It was a full two minutes, that seemed more like ten to Nayati, before another crack of a dry branch being trod on sounded in the silence.

A silhouette of a young man entered the small clearing that formed their camp. Niyol remained motionless and, although in the open, remained unseen at first. A second man and then a third appeared.

64

"Where is he then?" A gruff but adolescent voice spoke.

"If you are seeking me, then I am here before you." Niyol answered calmly.

The three men almost jumped out of their skin before turning to take in Niyol's silhouette.

"We're looking for the one called Nayati and you aint him. Where is he, tell us and you can go unharmed?"

"He is here and yet he is not here," Niyol stated.

"What's that supposed to mean?"

"It is as I say."

"Last chance old timer, tell us where he is, or you'll suffer."

"It is true that I cannot see him but beware of spirits that inhabit the land around here. Do not offend them for they can be swift to seek vengeance."

"What are you talking about? I've given you two chances to answer my questions and still you talk in riddles. Now you'll feel the pain that you and your kind deserve."

The first man threatened with a raised clenched fist. Before he could deliver the blow, an arrow thumped into the ground, inches from his foot. He halted and just stared at it. Two more followed in quick succession, each landing in front of the other two assailants.

"It is my thoughts that you have angered the spirits."

A blood-curdling screech, emitting from seemingly everywhere, sent shivers down the spines of each of the men who stood frozen.

Three more arrows, one in front of each man, hit the ground. The two behind the first turned and moved away leaving the first man alone in front of Niyol.

"You should leave," Niyol stated calmly, "for after the arrows come the slashing blades, as long as a man's arm. I have seen them only once, and the remains of what was once a man. You have angered the spirits and there is no forgiveness."

The man's face showed confusion as he mulled over what Niyol had said. The terrible screech came again, and the man's eyes widened. He turned and fled.

"I have never heard an angry spirit before Nayati, but if it was so, the sound you made, would strike fear in its heart."

Nayati returned from cover and grinned at his grandfather.

"I must try this screech on Doli."

"You will not Nayati. Tell me what you did to cause three men to follow you. They meant to harm you."

"I did nothing to them Old Man."

Nayati told Niyol everything that had transpired at the market and Niyol listened without interrupting. When he finished an uncomfortable silence hung over them whilst Niyol kept his grandson waiting.

"What is it that you learned from this?" the old man asked.

"You were right about the people who drink. They act without thought or reason."

Niyol nodded without expression.

"What else did you learn?"

"I am hated by some because I am of mixed spirits and yet they have no reason to hate me."

"There are those who hate difference."

"Why is this so?"

"People are not born with such hatred; they learn it from others. They fear those who are different, and those they do not understand. It is the same with other cultures also. Tell me grandson what was your response towards the boy I brought to our home?"

Nayati coloured, glad that the darkness concealed his sudden embarrassment. He paused before answering and ignored Niyol's last question.

"You do not hate me, and you are not of mixed spirits. Haloke does not hate me and she is not of mixed spirits."

"We see the person who is Nayati and do not fear you."

"Why is it that they do they not see me also?"

"They do not wish to."

"It is difficult to understand."

"We will talk more another time, for now I need to sleep. You will track those men so that we know they will not return, and you will make them move faster by making the noise."

Nayati grinned. This was his grandfather's way of saying that this was his mess and he should clean it up.

"It will be as you say Grandfather," Nayati said, and left the clearing.

There are advantages for being the old wise one. Niyol thought and smiled as he lay down again and shut his eyes.

Chapter 10
The Awakening

Doli watched her family disappear from view around the bend. At ease with solitude, she often tended the gardens alone from dawn to dusk, so isolation for a few days did not daunt her. She would take advantage of their absence and clean their home, as there was nobody to protest or get in her way and was looking forward to the task.

Except for the lack of food, the boy had received, and the subsequent thinning of his body, she was not too concerned about his physical well-being; his injuries were improving.

The swelling around his head wounds had subsided and healing was taking place. Any damage inside his head wouldn't become clear until he woke. The bruising was fading now, and all the lacerations sealed underneath the scabs.

The nose, Niyol had reset, showed no sign of ever being broken, what remained a mystery now, was when the spirits would release him.

She looked up into the sky above and saw, once again, the eagle circling high above.

"If you look out for him," she said aloud, "then you look out for me also!"

Then she heard the eagle's plaintive cry. She didn't know if it was a response or not but found it reassuring. It was the first time she'd heard it and it pleased her at its apparent agreement to the words she spoke.

Doli took the entire day to clean out the dwelling, trying not to raise too much dust that might choke her patient. Finishing, she set about making an evening meal, deciding to have the same broth she'd been feeding her patient with for the past few days, to save time and labour. She made some flat corn bread and lay it on the large flat stone by the hearth.

While she was feeding him, he made a sound. It was the first he'd made during his unconscious ordeal. He coughed, spluttering at the trickle of broth being administered to his mouth. Some of it oozed out, so Doli gently wiped it from his face, waiting for a few seconds before continuing with his meal.

"So, you return from the spirits," she said aloud, but with no response.

After clearing away their bowls, she moved her sleeping mat closer, in readiness for the night.

She stared down at the unconscious boy from where she stood, smelling the unmistakable mixture of the natural body odours and the salves she had applied for the healing process. She bathed him and reapplied the herbal medicines.

Fetching a bowl of fresh water and a soft cloth, she started. For the first time, she observed his body and face properly. The healing wounds were revealing the young man beneath. She noticed the long, slim but muscular legs and admired his torso, filling out with maturity and broadening at the shoulders, in the same way that she admired her brother's. From this, she guessed his age at being the same as her own, or perhaps a year older.

She stared at his face for longer than she would had he been awake. There was no mistaking the features of a Navajo Indian, but the detail was only just becoming apparent. His lips full, sensual, and the nose small and slender.

He was pleasing to look at, and she wished to see him with his eyes open. Gently peeling back an eyelid, she revealed the colour of his eyes; blue, but a much lighter shade than hers and her brother's, almost grey. They were eyes that suggested intelligence and that would perceive beyond the obvious.

His brow was prominent, offering a further suggestion of intelligence and the hair that flowed from his head was identical to hers and Nayati's; dark and straight, though shorter.

Lighter than her own, her skin seemed to accentuate his handsome features, and she found his face pleasant to look at. Something twisted deep inside her, compelling her to look for longer than would be acceptable in her culture. He differed from her brother, not as beautiful but harder, more masculine; she liked his face.

Finishing her task, she placed more wood on the fire and settled down for the night facing her patient. The rhythmic rise and fall of his chest as he breathed, soothed her. Then she looked at his face before she closed her eyes.

She slept undisturbed but woke to find that her patient had shifted position during the night. Pleased with this, she rose and prepared a light meal for herself and then administered water to her patient while it cooked.

Harvesting the last two garden plots of wheat ready for the winter, was her task today. It was her way, to go for the day, to cut and thresh the crop, then bundle the straw as fresh bedding for Friend.

Today she had an alternative plan. With her patient showing the early signs of waking, she did not want to leave him for too long. She would cut and bring back the crop, threshing it outside the cave. This would mean taking several trips, but they would keep her away for shorter periods.

She went outside, looked up, and smiled at the eagle above, knowing instinctively that she'd made the right decision. Away from the cave, she could see the eagle through the trees. Its presence was her security; its absence would warn her if something were wrong.

She made eight such trips to and from the two patches of wheat planted several hundred yards away. On each return she checked her patient, but he remained still and quiet.

Next, she pulled the ears of wheat from their stems and placed them in a large container. This she would leave for a few days, to allow the seed to fall off, but the ears were already ripe and the seed loose.

Then she used a shallow basket to toss the grain, allowing the breeze to blow the chaff away, leaving the seed ready for sacking and storing. This task took her several hours to complete until she heaved the grain container into the dwelling.

From time to time, she glanced upwards, reassured by the continuing presence of the eagle, soaring in lazy circles high above.

She took the straw, to an open structure; hidden from view and made from stout posts driven deep into the ground, with a canopy of living branches from the surrounding trees. Tied down some seasons ago, they had

71

continued to grow in their new positions. The natural roof of the structure was so thick that no light passed through it, masking that the structure was man made.

It was getting late as Doli stacked the bundles and made her way back to the cave but, although she felt tired, she was pleased with her day's labours. The evening passed in the usual way until she retired to sleep.

Noises coming from the bed beside her disturbed her slumber. She woke and raised herself on one elbow, and, by the flickering light of the dying fire, she saw the boy's head rolling from side to side. He moaned and cried out in pain, but she couldn't understand the words of his restless mutterings.

Rising, she wet a cloth and placed it on his forehead. His movement slowed. Then, gently raising his head with one hand, she held a cup to his lips and for the first time since she'd nursed him; he drank.

"Take just a little," she told him. "Not too much."

When he'd finished, she watched him return to sleep. Twice more during the night, the boy woke her and each time she made him drink. Once, he opened his eyes, staring with such intensity, but at something faraway in his mind before he fell into a deep, unmoving sleep.

In the morning, she wove a basket, but did not wish to leave her patient for too long, as she felt sure that he would wake soon. She collected her things from the storage room and sat crossed legged on the floor beside her patient.

An hour later he woke. He made no sound, or attempted movement, but lay watching Doli as she worked. When she glanced over to complete one of her frequent checks, Doli saw his eyes upon her. She dropped her basket in surprise but said nothing. Instead, she rose to fetch water and, raising his head as before, gently poured some into his mouth.

"Thank you," he said, his voice hoarse.

Doli nodded, at first unsure what to say, then enquired, "Have you pain?"

"Here, here and here," he replied, pointing to his ribcage, collarbone and the back of his head.

"Your injuries were many and you sleep with the spirits for many days," she told him, trying to avoid the penetrating gaze of his eyes.

"What happened to me?" he asked.

"That is for you to answer," she told him.

She stood and placed some broth to warm by the fire. Then taking a spoon, she returned to his side and knelt down.

"Eat," she commanded, feeding him the contents of the bowl. "Now rest and grow strong; the journey of healing will be long."

She returned to her basket and continued working while he watched, before his eyes closed and he slept.

He awoke in time for the evening meal that Doli was preparing. Again, he watched her silently while she worked.

"You wake, before I wake you!" she exclaimed. "It is time to drink and eat. You would sit up?"

He nodded his consent, so she placed her strong, gentle arms under his to raise him.

"If it pains you, I will stop," she assured him.

"It can't be worse than the pain in my head."

"You need to drink much water. Drink slow and the pain there will lessen."

He gritted his teeth and rode the waves of pain and nausea that swept through his body as she helped him to a sitting position. She fetched two sacks of grain for him to lean against, and passed him water, a plate of rabbit stew and some fresh made corn bread. He held the cup unsteadily, sipping as she'd instructed, balanced the food on his lap, took the spoon she offered and ate every morsel.

"That was good!" he said in appreciation, and she smiled, nodding at the compliment.

"How long was I unconscious?" he asked.

His voice was deep and melodic and Doli liked the way it sounded.

"Rest now; questions can be asked later," she said. He nodded a response as she removed the grain sacks and helped him to lie back once more.

She rose early the next morning, before the boy, and went about her usual daily duties before glancing over to see him watching her.

"My people do not look at another in such a way?" she stated, embarrassed at his scrutiny.

"Sorry, I didn't mean to stare! It is not every day that you wake to find somebody so beautiful caring for you!" he replied, smiling for the first time.

The smile transformed his face into a vision that appealed to her more than she could have imagined, and she could not help but smile back.

"It is not our custom, to be so familiar!" Doli stated.

This time it was his turn to feel embarrassed.

"I didn't mean to offend you," he offered an apology, "But I didn't exaggerate either."

"I will take it in the manner I think you mean," Doli responded graciously. "Today you will stand. Your legs have been still for too long, and the muscles will be weak," she continued, pleased when he agreed with an affirmative nod and no further comment.

Chapter 11:
The Eagle

Later that morning, Doli carried a sleeping mat and blanket outside and then the two sacks of grain she had used the evening before. Hearing the sharp cry of a bird, she glanced upwards to see that the eagle continued to patrol the sky. She muttered a small thank you for its guardianship and went inside to fetch her patient.

"The door is low, there is need to bend. It will cause pain," she informed him. "Stand first! You may feel sickness. Lean on me and I will bear some of your weight." Apprehensively, the boy nodded.

As she helped him up, he enjoyed the gentleness of her touch, feeling the strength that belied the slim figure standing beside him as he leant on her.

She reassured him that the strange feeling of weakness that consumed his body was normal and would soon pass.

"Walk around the cave first," Doli ordered.

He was glad for that instruction, as he wasn't certain of negotiating the door. They moved around in a gentle circle and Doli bore as much of his weight as she could, slowly reducing her support. After a few circuits she sensed his stability improving.

"This is a strange place," he remarked. "I've seen nothing like it before."

"Let your thoughts be on the task ahead," she admonished him. "There will be time for talking later."

He obeyed, enjoying the way she liked to control every situation.

She led him to the entrance. "Again, you may feel sick," she told him.

He noticed the 'again'; he hadn't admitted to feeling sick the first time! Bending over, he could not help gasping at the pain, but almost before he could stop, Doli had led him through and he stood upright. Then she led him towards the mat in the sunshine.

"I would like to walk a little more," he said, raising his eyebrows to seek her approval.

Doli nodded leading him around the open space that formed their front yard. She stopped short of the cliff edge and allowed him to absorb the vista.

He caught his breath at the beauty the sight. "It's the most amazing view I've ever seen. You can see for miles above the canopy."

"Yes, but in spring and autumn the clouds can eat it for many days," she responded, pleased with his response.

He continued to view the landscape, noticing how the deep-green canopy undulated with the terrain beneath, narrow gaps marking ravines and watercourses.

Doli stood and gazed with him for a short while, before leading him to his seat at the back of the clearing.

"Sit, feel the sun. I will bring food and water," the instruction clear and in a voice that said, don't argue.

She disappeared back into the cave and soon came back with breakfast. They ate silently and as soon as they had finished; she cleared away. When she returned, she sat cross-legged beside him.

"You have been waiting long and have many questions," she said, holding eye contact with him.

"I do; who are you? And where am I?" he started, without hesitation.

She smiled, "Listen, and I will answer this."

Her smile captivated him; it was strange how easy he felt in her presence.

"I am Doli of the Navajo, and this is my home. I live the life of a Navajo with my brother, Nayati, who came to this world on the same day. My grandfather, Niyol also. We live here since we were small, and I would choose no other place. My brother and grandfather will return soon after trading. Grandfather found you in the desert, close to death. He brought you here."

She paused, and he seized the opportunity to question further. "Your parents?" he asked.

"My parents died when I was small, in a car crash. We do not know who drove them from the road."

Her eyes showed a slight misting. "That must have been hard for you and your brother."

"Life was difficult, but Niyol came. He cares for us! There is no other as he." she said in a quieter voice.

They sat silently for a moment before Doli asked. "What name were you given? And why do you visit death in the desert?"

Before he answered, they heard the cry of an eagle and looked up.

"My Grandfather is thinking the eagle is your animal spirit. It has watched over you since before he found you," she told him.

They watched it soar above them. It was flying lower and still descending. It cried out again and again, and Doli shivered. "I think it warns us!" she said.

"How could you know this?" asked the boy, surprised.

"It has never flown this low, and I have heard its call only once."

An icy shiver passed through her body and she stood up. Her warning had penetrated his thoughts too. She walked around the clearing, and then round the bend beyond the rocks, but could see nothing untoward. She reappeared with a worried look on her face.

"What is it?" he asked.

She shook her head perplexed. "I do not know."

Suddenly, her hand flew to her mouth. "Do not move!" she commanded.

He looked at her, sensing her fear, and obeyed her instruction. "What is it?" he asked again.

She did not reply, but fixed her gaze at his eyes, forcing his attention.

Behind the boy inched a snake, its body long, sinuous and deadly; silent, until it shook its rattle. The boy heard the sound and turned his head towards it. He saw the distinctive pattern running down its scaly body. The head raised from the ground as it swayed gently back and forth, its forked, black tongue flickering as it tasted the surrounding air. His pulse rate rose, and he could hear his heart hammering in his ears. His breathing became laboured as his shallow gasps fought his painful ribs. Yet he could not move. The diamondback rattlesnake inched ever closer.

Calls from the eagle became louder as the bird dropped from the sky.

Four feet away now, the snake was within striking range; suddenly they both felt a rush of wind as the eagle, dark as a shadow, whipped past them at incredible speed.

It extended its legs and talons as it approached the ground and sunk them deep into the snake just behind its head. It rose again, wings straining, flying upwards higher and higher, over the canopy of trees they had admired earlier, with the snake dangling below. Soon it was a distance away from them and as they watched, the eagle released its prey to fall hundreds of feet below. They watched it, lost in stunned silence.

The eagle turned and flew back towards them, assuming its silent vigil above them once again.

Doli ran the short distance to the boy. "You are unhurt?" she asked.

"Yes, just shaken. How did you know of the danger? You hadn't even seen the snake to start with."

She looked perplexed. "The spirits warned me! It is so, the eagle is your animal spirit."

"I don't know about that, but that eagle saved my life for sure," he answered, his breathing coming back under control. He looked up and shouted. "Thank you, Great Bird!"

Doli sat down beside him once more, calm and ready to continue their conversation.

He sensed the change in her and admired her fortitude.

"What name do you answer to?" she asked him.

Misery masked his face. "I'm sorry," he said, "I'm sorry I cannot answer your question."

Doli did not reply, her expression inquisitive.

"I don't know my name, I don't know why I was in the desert, and I don't know where I'm from. I have no memories at all, before waking and seeing you."

There was a sadness about him as he became silent and his eyes stared out over the canopy.

Doli paused before answering. "It is of no matter; Grandfather has said someone hit you many times to the

79

head. Injuries to the mind, we thought it might be so, it is so that this is true. Your memories may return, but no one can say when. The spirits will decide this. Take comfort in knowing the eagle spirit will protect you until you heal."

The boy thought about this. She was so convinced and yet his mind was full of doubts. The eagle had saved his life though.

"I hope you are right, Doli. Having no identity is strange and I need all the help I can get. Your grandfather sounds like a wise man; maybe he can offer some words to aid my recovery."

"He is wise, and his understanding is strong. He will help you, for now, you need a name. I will give you a Navajo name that is right."

They remained silent for a few minutes, before Doli almost shouted. "Yiska! Yiska will be your name!"

"Yiska?" he questioned, "What does it mean?"

"It means; 'the night has passed'," she told him.

"I can see why you chose it! It is a good name, a name with meaning and I will adopt it for now!" he said pleased. "Yes! Yiska it is."

Chapter 12:
Spirit Dreams

That night Yiska retired early, tired from the day's physical exertions. It was too soon from Doli's perspective and she busied herself in the cave with a few cleaning chores.

Like any nurse, she checked her patient at regular intervals, aware that he'd exerted himself more than she would have liked him too, after such a long period of unconsciousness.

She smiled, as she looked at him for longer than she would have, had he been awake; aware that it wasn't just his physical attributes that appealed to her. He'd been respectful, and the calmness he'd displayed when he had admitted his memory loss showed strength. She would have found it difficult to be calm, in his place; and shivered at the notion.

Her thoughts turned to how her grandfather and brother would perceive him. Niyol would like him she thought, but her brother would be far more difficult to please; he would have doubts, reservations and even feel threatened by Yiska's presence. *Only time would tell, she mused pushing the thoughts aside.*

She finished her tasks and retired, looking forward to conversing with Yiska in the morning.

He slept until just before dawn when images invaded his dormant mind. It started with flashes of white light, featureless, but forceful enough for him to turn his head to one side at every individual flash. The light became persistent, shimmering like a desert mirage before, at the centre, a figure of a child materialised and floated gently towards him. A boy, his features unclear, but there was a familiarity about him he couldn't identify. Yiska reached out to him but as his arm approached the boy, the image retreated until he lost it in the haze. Yiska grunted in his sleep at the physical effort of reaching out and his sounds woke Doli who moved silently to his side.

Another shape, distant at first, materialised in his vision and floated towards him. Again, he reached out to touch, this time the forming image of a key. His hand inadvertently touched Doli on the shoulder and he retracted it, fingers closing on the key in his mind. She watched him with empathy believing he was having a nightmare. Yiska opened his fingers to examine the key but there was nothing there and its absence agitated him enough to call out against the loss.

The shimmering haze appeared again, and a third object formed, cuboid, seeming to hover, close enough for him to make out the shape but too distant for identification. Yet he recognised it, and as it too retreated into the distance, the need to have it made him sit up and reach out with both hands to get it. As it disappeared from his view, he cried out a desperate "Noooooo!" An eagle flew across his field of vision and disappeared, and he opened his eyes wide as he woke with a terrifying sense of despair and loss.

Doli grasped his hands and gently lowered them as his eyes focussed on the dim light in the cave coming from the dying embers of the fire. His breath exhaled a little too fast, and she saw the dream had caused him tension and unease. Holding on to his hand, she shushed him, as a mother would a newly born baby, and his breathing slowed to a more normal pace. She gave him a few more seconds before speaking.

"You dream walk with the spirits, but you have returned, are you calm now?"

"Yes, thank you, it was a bad dream."

"What did the spirits show you?"

Yiska noted her referral to the spirits and decided not to question her beliefs. Somehow, he knew that the Navajo people had powerful connections to, and beliefs in, the spirits of their religion, although he wasn't sure how he knew that.

"Images of objects that have no meaning and yet I felt a sense of loss as each disappeared."

"What were the objects?"

"One was an image of a boy, familiar and yet I did not recognise him, the image was misty. Then a key, I don't know what it belonged to, but it was mine. The third object never showed itself fully and I do not understand what it was. When that disappeared from view an eagle flew past and I woke up."

Doli passed him some water and told him to sip some.

"The Eagle woke you from your journey with the spirits and this I think was to protect you from the visions."

"Why would I need protection from my dreams?"

"Only the spirits have the answer to this."

She reached out and gently wiped a few beads of perspiration from his forehead with a small cloth.

"Can you rest, it is early to rise when there is no need to do so?"

"I don't think I could go back to sleep now; I am too awake."

"Then we shall sit together and talk and share a warm drink." Doli told him, assuming control of the situation.

Yiska smiled, liking the way she fussed over him, always seeming to know what he needed.

"You should speak to Niyol when he returns about your dream walk," she stated, as they sipped a warm, sweet brew that Yiska didn't recognise.

"It is so that dreams have meaning; Grandfather is wise and understanding of such things, he may have answers to your visions."

"I wouldn't want to bother him with such a trivial thing like a dream." Yiska responded, feeling a little embarrassed. "I would be happier if we could just forget it ever happened."

Doli nodded impassively.

"It will be as you say but if you change your thinking, he is wiser than any I have known."

Yiska changed the subject and asked her to tell him more about her grandfather and brother and as she talked, he recognised the deep love, respect and pride she voiced.

He lay back as she continued, listening to her strange way of speaking and the gentle tones in her voice and wondered if anybody had ever spoke about him in the same manner.

Afterwards, he asked her to come outside with him to watch the sunrise and she was content that he enjoyed the wonders of the outside world that she and her family also relished. Going outside, she prepared the area as she had yesterday in the same manner before returning and helping him up. He stood up, steadier on his feet now, and she stayed back a little as he made his way to the cave entrance and lowered his frame to pass through it.

Outside he sat unaided and Doli placed a thick blanket around his shoulders to offset the early morning chill before sitting alongside.

"The blanket is big enough to share," Yiska told her opening the blanket out.

Doli realised that he was inviting her to sit closer to him and felt her skin flush. Yiska noticed, but feigned ignorance as he held the blanket open and placed it around her shoulders as she followed his request. He smiled as he felt her closeness and breathed in the natural perfume of her body. Something tugged deep in his stomach, he didn't know what, but it felt good.

Neither spoke as they sat enjoying the changing shades of green in the canopy ahead of them caused by the intensifying light as the sun rose. Eventually, Doli announced that it would be a warm day with plenty of sun. Yiska didn't ask her how she could tell, already he knew that if she said it would be, then it would be.

"If it's a good day, then I would like to stay out here." Yiska told her.

"It is warm, and the sun is good for your spirit." Doli replied.

"I think that the beauty and peace of your home are also good for the spirit, I cannot imagine a more beautiful place to be."

"It pleases me that you think this of my home; it is so, we all feel this way. We have eaten many meals on this place that you sit, listening to the sounds of the forest."

"Grandfather taught Nayati and me many lessons about life here in the stories he tells. He will tell you many stories too, it is his way; it is how he passes on his great knowledge and wisdom. When we listen to him, we learn how to see and hear all around us."

"I will look forward to hearing what he teaches."

"He will teach you the ways of the Navajo and when the spirits return your memories, you will tell us of the ways of your people if that pleases you."

"I would like that," Yiska told her gratefully.

He reached out and placed his hand on hers. Doli pulled hers sharply away.

"Our people do not touch in such ways."

"I'm sorry, I did not mean to offend, I wanted to say thank you for the way you've cared for me."

Yiska's face turned a vivid shade of red and he wished he could move quick enough to get away before she saw his embarrassment. Doli turned her face to his and Yiska could not turn from her gaze.

"I too am sorry for I did not understand the meaning behind the touch. It is good to have your skills recognised, and I am pleased for this. I did not mean to make you feel as you do."

Yiska smiled. "I think I need those lessons with your Grandfather," he said, and she smiled her response.

They passed the rest of the morning gently with Doli telling a few stories of her own and answering his questions about the various birds and small creatures that he heard or saw. Her knowledge impressed him, there was nothing in this beautiful place she did not know about in great depth. He only hoped that he could do her justice when his memories returned.

Doli didn't mind his temporary failings though, already any doubt about him had long since dissipated, and she felt confident that he was a good person.

There was his eagle spirit too; that such a bird guarded him was a good omen and would bring security for them all as long as it stayed above. She glanced up seeing it locked in its never-ending circles on thermals of warm air rising from the mountains below.

Chapter 13:
Yiska

The following day, at mid-afternoon, Niyol and Nayati rounded the rock pile bend, and were home once more. Doli and Yiska were still sitting where they'd been at dawn that day, her position partly obscuring Yiska from their view. Niyol registered the eagle above her before he spotted their guest sitting beside his granddaughter.

Doli leapt to her feet and threw herself at her grandfather, in a hug that suggested that they might have been apart for several months, instead of a few days. She released him, moving to her brother to repeat the greeting. Making no move to help him, despite knowing that the boy must be in pain, Niyol watched his guest struggle to his feet.

Yiska approached Niyol and held out his hand, in the ways of the western world, and Niyol received, and shook it.

"Hello, you must be Niyol; I have heard a lot about you, sir. It's good to meet you," he greeted.

Niyol nodded. "It pleases me that you are back from the spirits. What name do you answer to?" he asked.

"I am Yiska."

Niyol smiled and then continued. "You have slept with the spirits I am thinking; the name is right for you."

"Your granddaughter chose it, sir."

"Nayati, come greet our guest," Niyol commanded, saving his grandson from the affections of his sister.

Nayati approached, his greeting cool, his face impassive. He stood, as upright as possible in front of the boy and stared eye to eye. Nayati was about two inches taller. To his surprise, Yiska matched his stare in the same direct, unflinching manner.

"I am Nayati, Grandson of Niyol of the Navajo," he said coldly, without releasing the grip of his eyes.

"I am Yiska," the boy replied, still meeting Nayati's stare.

Niyol stepped forward, "Nayati see to Friend, that we may sit and rest a while."

Nayati turned to his grandfather and nodded. "It will be as you ask, Grandfather."

"Yiska, forgive me, while I see to our supplies," Niyol said.

"May I offer my help, sir?"

Niyol blinked in disbelief. "Your offer is thoughtful," he replied.

"My patient will return to his seat before he does more harm to his injuries," Doli interjected.

Niyol smiled. "It will be as you ask, Granddaughter!" he agreed, his eyes twinkling with amusement at her forthright nature.

Yiska looked at her with surprise but decided not to argue.

While Niyol and Nayati tended to their tasks, Doli cooked a meal. It was a little earlier than their usual eating time, but she had anticipated their hunger from their travels. She decided that they would eat outside as there was still warmth in the day, and it would save Yiska moving more than necessary.

Nayati glanced over to the boy each time he took a load into the cave, but Yiska just stared out over the treetop canopy. It wasn't long before they'd finished their tasks and Doli called them over to eat. They ate their meal in silence with both Nayati and Doli eating quicker than usual, in their haste to tell the stories of the past few days. Niyol observed Yiska eat as slowly as he did and knew he still had a long period of recovery ahead.

When the meal ended, Doli insisted that her brother be first to tell of their journey. With detail, to the same extent as Niyol would have used, he started. They listened patiently before Doli questioned him about the people he'd met and talked with. He presented Doli with the necklace he had traded for, which she adored saying what a resourceful and thoughtful brother he was. Niyol knew that his grandson left out the part about seeking the girl's help and said nothing about the evening's entertainment he'd attended. The old man refrained from the opportunity to tease.

Then it was Doli's turn. She took her time and retold the events of the last two days, enjoying the attention focussed upon her. When she'd finished, there was a silence before Niyol began.

"It is an honour to gain knowledge of the spirit animal that walks with you on life's journey. Many wait for years to learn of their totem; some never discover this. Nayati and Doli still wait to find theirs. The eagle is powerful, and it means your journey will be long and hard, Yiska."

"I am honoured sir, and I will not forget what the bird did for me," Yiska started, but Niyol interrupted.

"It is right that you speak in this respectful manner, as your customs demand. Here we live as Navajo in the traditional ways. It will please me if you call me Niyol, for that is the name my parents gave me, it honours them for people to call me so."

"It is clear, someone has brought you up in the ways of the western world, you may not have knowledge of Navajo ways. I see Navajo in your face, as I see it in my grandchildren. The colour of your skin and eyes, like theirs, tell me that you are of mixed spirits. You have a parent from each tribe. It is not yet clear how long you will stay with us but as your body heals, I will teach you some of our ways."

"You are generous, Niyol; I would like this; I will listen and learn fast. Since I have little knowledge about either culture it would be good to learn a little about one of them at least."

Nayati fumed at this; all his life he'd been his grandfather's student and did not relish losing any of the attention he was used to.

It was as if Niyol sensed this, and he added.

"Nayati and Doli will help with this, for they have skills from many years of practice."

Yiska had been watching his hosts carefully since dinner. He didn't miss the annoyance on Nayati's face, nor the smile of delight on Doli's. It was no surprise that he'd taken an instant liking to Niyol, already deciding to try hard to honour their ways. It was the only way he could show gratitude for their kindness.

"Niyol, you saved my life in the desert and I'm grateful. I have little to offer but would be pleased to do anything that helps any of you," he said.

Niyol replied, "It is right to be thankful, but do not burden yourself with this debt. It is a man's duty to respect and guard all life. Your spirit guide led me to you, and it is this you should honour."

They sat silently before heading into the cave and the warmth of the fire. The evenings were drawing in earlier, and the temperature getting cooler as late autumn approached. Soon the first snows would cleanse the landscape and bury the autumn colours in a veil of white.

Niyol had noticed the boy struggle through the entrance and again his effort to mask the pain. He too had been examining everyone's body language and facial expressions.

He's strong, shows respect and sees within. Doli, draws his attention, but that is of no surprise. There may be trouble with him and Nayati. Nayati is jealous, unhappy with his presence; I will speak with him, and soon. The old man's thoughts raced.

Niyol asked Yiska some probing questions about his life before the injury, to see if he could jolt any of the lost memories, and he could sense the boy's misery at not being able to recall anything. He placed himself in the boy's shoes, trying to imagine what it would be like to have no identity; but he could not. *It was clear; the spirits have sent him to us for a reason. We may have a part in his journey, he mused.*

Thinking too about the eagle spirit, he wondered what journeys lay ahead of the boy. There had been no exaggeration in his words about the powerful strength of the spirit.

He deliberated about the silent, respectful nature of the boy too. Was this his normal disposition, or was he trying to adapt with the situation in which he found himself and to those around him?

Since he spoke in the Western way, he doubted he had much knowledge of the traditional ways. There was Navajo in him, from one or other of his parents and therefore it was right to teach him about the Navajo ways.

91

But what about his parents? So many unanswered questions! He sat absorbed in his thoughts, oblivious to the passing of time.

Doli sat silent, thoughts crowding her mind too. She had seen her brother's face; body language played such a huge part in their culture. She'd sensed his discomfort but could not work out the reasons for it but was glad that Niyol had laid a path for them to follow. She would enjoy her part in it.

A new companion, to talk to and share the things that made her life content, was good. It would be different here now, and she hoped Yiska would stay.

The eagle's presence worried her though. That it was still here suggested that its protective duties were yet unfinished, and she wondered what would happen that required more than the protection offered by her family. Despite her worries, she was glad of its continuing presence, especially, after experiencing its behaviour the day before.

Nayati's thoughts were black. Although he trusted his grandfather's wisdom, he could not understand the generosity that lay behind his offer. *This boy is of no importance to us, he thought. We risk our safety and home with him here. Who knows what he will do or say when he leaves, which he will do when he recovers from his injuries? What is it that Niyol sees in him? He dishonours my sister in the way he looks at her, more than with gratitude for the nursing! Why must I teach him our ways? He will not be thankful; our skills take years to learn! Then he will leave and forget all this, when he returns to his own world.* Nayati continued to brood.

Yiska's thoughts were much more positive. He could not believe his luck at the way they'd treated him. These people were sensitive and gentle by nature, yet he could sense incredible strength and fortitude. To live in the manner, they did was an achievement itself, and already he was warming to their ways.

Niyol was ancient, with a lifetime of experiences to draw from. Learning from him would be good, and he was looking forward to the prospect. He wondered if he had a grandfather of his own somewhere and hoped that he would be like Niyol.

Then his attention turned to Doli. She was beautiful, considerate and thoughtful, and he felt something new towards her; strange and yet comforting. He enjoyed her presence and was at peace when he was with her, liking the way she talked; the strange order in which she placed her words, and her Navajo accent.

Nayati was different though. He sensed a distance between them, which would be difficult to breach. It disappointed him! Deciding there and then, he would work hard to impress him and, whenever he could, try to match Nayati's skills. He felt sure that they could become friends and enjoy the companionship that only teenage boys could.

Over the next few weeks, Yiska regained his strength and his body recovered from its injuries.

During that period, he spent a lot of time with Niyol, listening carefully to the stories he told and working out their hidden meanings; he even tried to adapt his speech to match theirs. He gave everything thought before he undertook a task and did not shy from taking further advice. Doli often provided that advice, but despite his attempts to involve her brother, Nayati maintained his distance, or made excuses that he was too busy to help. Niyol noted all the interchanges without comment.

Chapter 14: Rivalry

One morning Niyol asked Yiska how his ribs and collarbone were.

"As good as new!" Yiska told him, whereupon Niyol examined him with firm fingers.

"You are right," he told him. "And your head?"

"The wounds have healed."

"I did not make myself clear. How are you inside your head?"

Yiska looked a little surprised by the question and paused before answering. The old man studied his face.

"There's a lot of confusion inside my head. I don't know who I am, who I was, where I come from, what is waiting for me when I return; where and who do I return to? Are there people who care for me, what if there is nobody to return to? I don't have a hint of an answer to these questions and it doesn't feel good."

The old man paused before answering.

"There is much you are uncertain of, but this is what I know Yiska. What you have said, there are many ways to feel about them. Answers are hidden from you. Live each day, do not worry about such things. Answers will come when the spirits return your memories. They will know when to allow this and, in this way, you will be ready for them."

"So, I should stay here for longer even though I have healed."

"This place calms in a manner that no other does. If you are to heal, it is my thinking it will happen here."

"You've already been kind and generous Niyol."

"There is much more to teach you Yiska, give this matter no more thought, for now you must learn skills needed for survival here in the mountains. The first snows are late this year, I fear that winter may be harsh when it arrives."

He called Nayati over to them.

"Nayati, fetch your bow and arrows; we must teach Yiska to use one!"

He explained that, although they owned a rifle, the noise could travel for many miles and they did not wish to draw attention to themselves.

Nayati fetched his bow and stood before his grandfather. Niyol took it, aimed and fired at a tree twenty yards away. It struck with a dull thud. He returned the bow to Nayati, instructing him further.

"Show Yiska the skill he needs, for good hunting."

Nayati loaded an arrow and aimed at the one protruding from the tree. He released the bowstring, and the arrow buried itself into the tree less than an inch from Niyol's own.

"Great shot Nayati!" exclaimed Yiska, impressed.

Nayati ignored him and fired two more, in quick succession, with the same accuracy. He held the bow out to Yiska, scorn apparent on his face.

Despite the sour look, Yiska could not help but appreciate Nayati's skill.

"It must have taken you a long time to have become this good and you must have practised a lot." Yiska voiced.

Nayati didn't answer so Yiska took it, loaded another arrow, aimed and fired. It too, hit the tree, about twelve inches from the others.

Niyol nodded his approval. "You show some promise, Yiska," he announced. "Nayati, teach Yiska to be as accurate as you!"

"But grandfather what about...?"

"There will be time enough for that later, Nayati," he admonished the boy, and Nayati's face fell as he realised there would be no escaping the situation.

For the next hour Nayati found fault with everything that Yiska did. At each shot he would criticise the technique Yiska used and each time Yiska made the changes he thought necessary, to have another fault pointed out. He endured the frustration, silently.

By the end of the practice, he'd improved; his arrows were now within six inches of the target each time. But the improvement was from his own tireless practice, rather than Nayati's reluctant guidance.

Niyol saw it all, experiencing mixed feelings. Irritated by his grandson's behaviour, but pleased with how Yiska had responded, he smiled as Yiska thanked his grandson for the expert advice and accredited him for his improvement. Nayati nodded curtly and stalked off into the forest. A relieved Yiska picked up his bow and practiced once more.

Niyol just smiled.

Doli had taken it upon herself to walk in the forest with Yiska each day, venturing further at each visit to build up his strength. She taught him to see the forest as a Navajo does, pointing out plants good for eating, healing and flavouring. She showed him wildlife, which he would

96

otherwise pass by, and the tiny trails the ground creatures had made.

The walks had ceased to be for the improvement of his health but were now because she enjoyed his company and answering the many questions he asked.

During one walk, he asked her why her brother had taken such a dislike to him. She replied that she was sure that he did not dislike him but feared the consequences to the family's security if others were to hear about their existence, on the mountain. She also suggested that he would not like to become close to someone and then lose that friendship when Yiska left. Yiska told her he couldn't go back to a society he was ignorant of, and one that had mistreated him. After a moment's thought, she responded by reminding him that it was not a society that had caused his injuries, but a person or persons.

"Not all people would treat you in this way, but I understand how you feel," she added.

Yiska let the topic drop.

Later that day, Nayati returned with two fresh rabbits. Yiska nodded at him but received no response. Niyol looked on impassively.

Inside the cave, he gave the kill to Doli who took the rabbits, praising his hunting skill.

"Nayati!" Yiska called when he came back outside, "I wish to challenge you!"

The Navajo looked up and walked towards him. "What is this challenge you speak of?" he enquired.

"I need to test my fitness, and you are the fittest of us all," Yiska replied, flattering Nayati's ego. "I have seen how swiftly you chase your prey in the forest when you hunt and wonder if you're as fast over distance."

Nayati adopted a scornful look. "You will lose," he said, "But I take your challenge."

Nayati chose the course, to a fallen tree they both knew on the other side of the mountain and back, a distance of about five miles.

Niyol called Doli to start the race. She picked up a feather up from the ground.

"When the feather touches the ground, you will start!" she ordered.

She released it and both boys glued their eyes to it as it floated to the ground; both ready to start the second it landed, neither seeking an unfair edge.

Niyol and Doli glanced at each other as they sprinted away.

"The result of this race may bring problems," Doli said to Niyol.

"It could bring or end problems," he replied. "Yiska is strong and does not rush into things without thought, but your brother thinks little before accepting the challenge."

"Nayati will not like to lose to Yiska," she continued.

"That is true; but it is so that a man must learn he is small in the ways of the world, and needs more than strength alone," he responded.

"I wish I could see the race," said the girl, her excitement apparent.

"I wish for that too, Granddaughter," Niyol grinned.

As the boys raced off, Nayati took the lead and set a furious pace. Yiska had expected him to do that and followed at a steadier rate, but never letting him out of sight.

"See me fly, Yiska, watch me fly from sight! Do not let the dust of my flight fill your mouth!"

Yiska could not help but grin. "You are still in my vision Nayati! Be careful I do not pass you when you tire!" he called back.

"There is little chance of that, for I am as swift as the eagle that watches over you!" Nayati was grinning as well for, although confident of winning, he was still enjoying the competition.

After two miles they approached a small stream easy to jump. Nayati slipped in the mud at the edge, losing his footing. He stumbled but did not fall. It cost him his advantage though for, as he restarted, Yiska was running alongside.

Yiska goaded him. "It is not enough to be swift; you must be sure-footed too!" he laughed.

Nayati glowered at the insult and sped up once more, but Yiska maintained his steady pace. Nayati rounded the fallen, hollow tree that marked the far end of the course and grinned as they passed in opposite directions. Yiska grinned back.

"I am just behind you!" he said

"But not close enough!" yelled Nayati.

Halfway back, Nayati tired from the pace he had set. Yiska gradually closed the gap as Nayati slowed down.

"Here I am Nayati!" he called out, within two yards of him.

"You will not pass me," Nayati said, speeding up again. This time Yiska also quickened and maintained the short gap between them.

"I will time it just right Nayati; you will not see me before I pass you," he panted.

"You sleep too long with the spirits!" came the reply.

Just before the end of the race, Yiska drew level with Nayati's shoulder who, despite his best efforts, could not pull away.

Niyol declared the outcome a tie. Nayati crouched down to recover his breath whilst Yiska fetched the water carrier. He returned and offered it to Nayati first, with a big grin on his face.

"You are as swift as the eagle, Nayati!" he offered.

Nayati took the water but did not respond or return the grin. Yiska could not help being disappointed that the communication they'd shared in the race had ended.

Niyol looked at Yiska and gestured for him to sit beside him. Yiska accepted, always happy to be in the old man's company.

"Tell me about the race!" he commanded.

Yiska related the details.

"Why is it you choose to run for your challenge? I have seen none as quick of foot as Nayati?"

"I do not know why I chose to run Teacher, it seemed a good way to compete on equal terms."

Yiska had now called the old man 'Teacher' as a sign of respect, and Niyol enjoyed his new title.

"Nayati is good at everything he does! I can run, and I thought it was a fairer challenge than archery

"This is true in matters of strength and endurance, but he has much to learn of other things," Niyol replied.

"I thought we connected at some level in the forest," said Yiska.

"Things take time, the nature of one man is different to another. You did not leave him behind at the end of the race, why is that so?"

"I did not want to make him feel bad in defeat, I wanted him to see that I deserve better than the way he has been treating me."

"You have patience beyond most others. Keep on that path and it will reward you in time."

"Thank you, Teacher, I will do my best."

Their conversation ended and Niyol smiled warmly at him. He was becoming fond of the boy, of the way he conducted himself and the way he persevered. They sat as companions.

Doli came across to them.

"Your strength is there for all to see. What challenge will you set Nayati next?" she asked.

"I think it more likely that Nayati will challenge me next, as he didn't win this one," Yiska answered, looking for confirmation from Niyol, who just smiled.

Chapter 15:
The Picnic

The next day Doli announced her intention to collect some medicinal herbs before the first snows concealed everything from view. She'd used most of her stockpile during her nursing of Yiska and some were difficult to find. Yiska offered to go with her, secretly relishing time away from Nayati's constant scorn and having more time alone with Doli. He told her he was keen to learn about the herbs and plants that healed his wounds and she promised to share her knowledge with him. Pleased that he wanted to come, she suggested that they packed some food as her chosen place was a fair distance away.

"It's called a picnic," Yiska explained.

Doli looked surprised. "It is so that a picnic passes time without work, it is for pleasure?"

"That's true, but it is possible to combine the two things. The work part is the searching for and gathering of the herbs whilst the pleasure part is the walk and the company." Yiska explained.

"It pleases me to join two things in this manner. We will make it so."

Yiska looked pleased. There hadn't been many opportunities where he'd been able to teach any of them anything.

Doli packed some flat bread, some late seasonal leaves and some fresh meat and then told Niyol of her intentions. He quizzed her on the area she intended to collect from and her chosen route. It was their custom that if any of them journeyed, they would share such details in case of accident or foul weather.

"You are taking the emergency pack with you granddaughter?"

"You know me better than to ask such a question Old Man, but you honour me with the care you show for me."

"Instruct Yiska on the contents of the pack and pass to him your knowledge of the healing plants in the pouch. There may be a time when he is in need of this.

"It will be as you say Old Man," she smiled warmly at him, and he could not help himself from returning it.

She took the matter further than her grandfather's request, showing Yiska all the contents of the pack. The amount of different plants included in such a small package surprised him. Showing him how to tie the bundle up and use the ties to form a shoulder strap, he took it from her as she already carried the food, water and a canvass bag for the fresh herbs and the two of them left. Nayati scowled, turning away and muttering something about woman's work.

Surprised at the pace Doli set, the comfortable conversation between the two of them ceased as he concentrated on trying to remember unique features to mark their route. He had often heard one of them describing a trek they were taking by using the natural features of the land and he wanted to learn to do the same. After an hour Doli slowed, informing him that they were close to where she expected to find one herb she needed.

"Look for a plant this high," she said, bending and lowering her hand to about a foot above the ground.

"The leaves will be round, as big as my hand; they feel as if covered with oil but are not."

"Waxy you mean?"

"If that is what I said," she said, with a little apprehension toward the unknown word he'd used.

Yiska smiled and nodded.

"It will have waxy leaves," she stated, smiling back.

A sudden recognition of her beauty made his mouth dry, as it had at random moments before. Swallowing the thought, he wondered why it happened at potentially embarrassing moments. She was beautiful though! He focussed his mind on the plant they sought, glad that she couldn't read his mind and that she remained oblivious to his feelings. Fortunately, her concentration was on the task in hand and he felt relieved.

Finding the plant before her, he smiled in pleasure, as she showed him how to pick the youngest leaves towards the top of the plant.

"I take just a few from each plant so that it can recover and grow fresh leaves. It is so that I hang them to dry, then rub them on a stone to make powder. This plant stop cuts and sores from going bad."

Yiska nodded and stored away his newly gained knowledge. They found a dozen more plants before Doli announced they had enough, and it was time to search for the next plant. Their pace increased again until they came to the area associated with it. They continued throughout the morning in the same manner until Doli suggested it was time to eat.

Yiska spotted a fallen tree laying across the animal trail they'd been following and suggested they use it as a bench. The sun was shining through a gap in the canopy and bathed the fallen trunk in its warmth.

Before long they were munching on their food, sitting next to one another and watching the sway of the surrounding forest. Occasionally, Doli would point to an unseen spot in the distance, telling Yiska there was something there. Yiska nodded but, try as he might, often he could not see what she was pointing to. Usually, it was a bird using foliage to cover its presence but revealing its location by singing.

They didn't speak while they ate but the conversation between them started once they'd finished.

Doli told him of the names and habits of the different birds and amazed him with her depth of knowledge.

"Do you ever do something for fun, just for fun?"

"There is little time for fun, there is always much to do."

"You should make time for fun; it doesn't have to be for long periods but can break up long periods of work."

"Tell me more about fun, what fun could we have here?"

"We could race through the forest like I did with your brother, but that would be too energetic. I know what..."

Yiska removed himself from his seat and walked over to a small patch of grass. He lay down flat on his back and stared upward.

"What is it you are doing?" Doli asked him.

"Come and lie beside me and I will explain."

Doli left the trunk and followed his example laying down next to him in the same manner.

Yiska felt her proximity, he could feel the warmth emanating from her body and her scent was like a magnet drawing him to her; he'd experienced it a few times and liked the security of it. Remembering the time, he'd touched her hand, and the way she had reacted to it, worried him. No longer able to move without contact, he didn't want to upset her and focussed on the task in hand.

"I will ask again Yiska, what is it you are doing?"

"I am watching the clouds."

"What is the meaning for this?"

"If you look hard at them, you can sometimes see faces or shapes that are like other creatures. Look at that one," he said carefully raising his arm and pointing. "What can you see?"

"I see a shape that looks like a petal from a flower in the forest I know."

"Good, you're getting the idea. Look towards the middle, there is a grey area shaped like a head. It hasn't got a face, but it has as many lines as Niyol's."

Doli giggled and then checked herself.

"This does not show respect to my Grandfather; we should not laugh at the lines of great age on his face."

"He would agree and laugh with us. It shows respect because we see him and not somebody else."

"I am not sure this is right, but I know what you say. If you look for something of me, what would it be?"

The directness of her question surprised Yiska, and he contemplated it.

"There's plenty that would remind me of you, but mostly I would look for your hair."

Doli looked bemused. "Why my hair?"

"I like the way it bounces when you walk, the way it swings when you turn your head and the way the sun shines through it."

Doli looked surprised and then pleased.

106

"I like it that my hair pleases you she said and smiled her most captivating smile."

Yiska returned the same question back.

"If I see a deer fawn in the cloud, it will tell me of your gentleness. If I see a mountain lion on the hunt, it would tell me of your patience. You are like a beaver building a dam too, you do not walk from a task or challenge."

"It pleases me that you see all these things too." Yiska replied, using her turn of phrase.

They spent the next twenty minutes trying to see, and often just imagining different things in the clouds. He made her laugh several times and realised that he hadn't heard it much before. She smiled but rarely laughed. He liked her laugh; it made him reciprocate.

Soon it was time to start the return journey, and they fell in step together and once again Doli set a fast pace.

"Doli, slow down. We need not walk so fast. It is possible to see the walk as fun too. This is a beautiful place, let's look harder and see more of what you showed me this morning."

"It will be as you say. I will show you more of the secrets hidden in the forest."

She fell in step with Yiska's pace and skipped to match his feet movement. Their hands touched several times as they walked. At first Yiska ignored it, pretending that it never happened but after a while he became so concerned that he increased the gap between them. Doli reacted by decreasing the gap and their hands touched again. Yiska stopped.

"If we walk this close to each other, then our hands will keep touching and I seem to remember that you don't like contact of this sort."

Doli suddenly understood why he'd kept moving apart. She'd thought he was just moving past or around something.

"When you held my hand before I did not know you. It is not good in our ways for this to happen unless with family. You are like family but not like family; the words for this I do not know. I like it that our hands touch, but others would frown on it."

"By others you mean Nayati?"

"More than Nayati, it is not the way of the Dineh."

"The Dineh?"

"It means 'the people'. They are Navajo and Apache, they are the Dineh."

"So, although we like our hands to touch, we could not do it when others are with us?" Yiska asked, with more than a hint of hope.

"It is difficult. It is not our ways and yet I wish it to be so. If we touch hands, then I go against our ways. No one will see this, but I will know. If I do not touch with your hand, then I will not feel as happy. I will speak to Grandfather later on this matter."

"It is a hard choice Doli and you must do what you feel is right."

Doli smiled and took Yiska's hand in hers.

"I would like it if you held my hand as we walk."

"I would like it too." Yiska said and adjusted their connection by holding her small delicate hand in his as gently as he could. She adjusted it interlocking their fingers.

"I will not break!" she said, with an almost teasing smile.

Yiska flushed but kept his head up and faced forward. Again, Doli smiled but this time without the teasing element. They resumed their walk and Doli his lesson on the gifts of the forest.

Chapter 16:
First Snow

Winter arrived that night as the four of them slept. The temperature plummeted and a light dusting of snow had settled gently on the mountain, dulling the late autumn colours, but not shrouding them completely.

Yiska awoke early, sensing something different. At the cave entrance a sliver of white light shone down the side of the covering where the blanket seal failed its purpose. There was a muffled silence. Accustomed to the silence of their domain, this was more spiritual, as if the spirits had suspended life.

Rising, he walked to the entrance, removed the cover and looked outside. The thin layer covering the ground enticed him out of the cave and he looked around, seeing the soft, white blanket covering the trees, caressing each branch and twig. As he moved forward, he looked out over the canopy below. There was little evidence of snow. With the temperature below one or two degrees higher, the snow must have fallen there as rain.

He returned to the cave, to make Doli a warm drink for when she woke. She performed that task every day for each of them and he would enjoy showing his appreciation for her consideration to their comfort.

As he turned, he faced Niyol who'd appeared silently behind him.

"Did you sense it Yiska?" he asked.

"The minute I woke, I was aware something was different," replied Yiska. "I could hear it, smell it."

"It is the first visit of winter! It is too soon, there is still much to do. Winter brings hard times; food is not in plenty, there are times we cannot go far, so spend much time in the cave," he informed, a serious look on his face. "You are becoming one with the place you live Yiska, you sense change before you see it and that is good."

Yiska smiled. "I am grateful for your teachings, Niyol. You've been so generous in everything you've done and continue doing. I'm glad that I can use what you have taught me," Yiska responded.

"It is the way that learning takes a lifetime. You have a difficult path ahead; this I know because your animal spirit stays close," Niyol added, looking up to the sky to see the eagle above.

"I'm prepared to face whatever life has to offer; thanks to each of you I'm fit and strong and have gained new knowledge. You've all become like family and I know that leaving will be a hard choice to make. If my memories don't return, I'll have to go, but for now, I would continue travelling my path with each of you, if you'll allow me to stay."

Niyol smiled at Yiska's choice of words and the way he said them.

"You will stay until you leave."

They returned to the cave and Yiska made them all a drink.

Nayati looked across, scorn on his face and asked, "Why do you do woman's work?"

Yiska thought carefully before answering. "Is it woman's work when you camp out overnight or if you are a journey?" he answered, with his own question.

"That is the way of survival," Nayati shot back.

"Our life here is survival too!" Yiska stated.

"Yes, Doli takes care of such things," Nayati answered, expecting that to be the end of the conversation.

Yiska changed his approach. "Why did you buy Doli that necklace on your trading journey?"

Nayati's eyes flashed his anger. "I wished to give her something; she was not there because of you,"

"Is it wrong of me to want to do something nice for Doli too?" Yiska finished.

Nayati did not respond but walked outside. Niyol watched his student. *It would appear there is more than one teacher here! he thought.*

Doli thanked Yiska for the considerate thought which, at first, passed by without her noticing, since he'd made drinks for all.

"It is nothing compared with the kindness you have shown me." Yiska replied.

"Teacher, may I ask you a question?" Yiska asked Niyol, later that evening.

"Speak! What is it you wish to know?"

"This place; the place we call home. Where is it? Why are we so secretive and protective about it? And why are there no others nearby?"

"That is many questions! But it is right that you know so you can protect it too," Niyol started. "We live in a place that western people call a National Park. They guard this area with fences and rule that no man can live here. They say they own the land and save it for their children.

"The people of the Navajo say this cannot be so. No man can own the land; it was here before men came into the world and will remain here after they go to the spirits. The Navajo respects the land and the creatures that live on it. We do not destroy it, for it is our duty to look after it. Our home in this park is most distant from the fences. I have seen no other person close to here. If they find us, they will make us leave," Niyol finished, and Yiska nodded his understanding.

When Nayati came back inside, Niyol announced that they must hunt meat to store for winter.

"We will hunt and fish each day, until we have what we need," he expounded. "At this time of year, the animals are slower and leave obvious tracks. It is easy to set traps. We will dry meat and fish and store some in salt. Already we have dried herbs and have plenty of grain. Vegetables will be few. We can freeze the crops we harvest, if there is much snow, and the temperature is low. They will keep fresh for many weeks. We must keep them in the ground as long as possible. It is hard in winter if the snow stays late into the spring."

Then after a brief pause. "We will leave tomorrow."

As soon as he had finished speaking, they set about collecting the equipment they needed for the hunt.

Chapter 17:
The Hunt

Niyol decided, as fishing was to be the focus of the hunt, they would journey down the mountain to a fast-flowing river to set traps and nets. Nayati and Niyol would use a spear with three barbed prongs. They could be thrown in the same way as a conventional spear, for short distances, or used as a stabbing tool in shallower water.

Because of the length of the journey, they would sleep out overnight and use Friend with the litter to carry their camping supplies and hunting equipment.

On route to the river, Niyol and Nayati would set snares for rabbits and ground squirrels. Made from animal sinew and twisted into strong cordage, they would easily hold any catch until they returned to the cave. Niyol explained that these formed a large part of their meat diet during winter, along with fish from the river. In warmer periods they would venture further down the mountains to hunt for deer.

Nayati placed rocks at the entrance of the cave to seal it, and they were ready to leave. They walked silently and Yiska noticed that little of the snow had made it through the canopy so travelling should be comfortable.

Niyol and Nayati stopped to examine the forest floor and set traps where evidence of a rabbit or squirrel was apparent. Yiska watched with interest as Niyol showed him how to recognise the signs. At each place where they set a trap, they marked the side with a small piece of leather attached tied to a stick. Nayati would remember them without the need to mark, Niyol too. Still, some would go unfound upon their return, marking reduced the number lost. It also highlighted their presence if a heavy fall of snow covered the traps.

Niyol instructed Nayati to show Yiska how to set the snares. This he did without patience, but Yiska learned and was soon helping.

Later that day, Niyol suggested Yiska work with Doli to set fish traps while he and Nayati used the spears. It was important to lay traps in the right places and Doli excelled at that. Fish was often the only meat they had left in late winter, so the more traps they set, the better they would catch and subsequently eat.

It pleased Yiska to be alone with Doli. So often he spent long periods of time under Niyol's guidance or at the mercy of Nayati's impatient and often inadequate instruction.

Still, he wished that the relationship between Nayati and himself would improve, and that Nayati would accept him. But he guessed the reasons for Nayati's behaviour were many, including the fact that he disliked the close relationship between him and Doli. He also suspected that Nayati was jealous of the time he spent with her too, and that he dishonoured her, although how, he didn't understand. Acceptance from Nayati would not come easily.

They reached the river with just two hours of daylight remaining and made camp near to the river's edge. Untethering the litter from Friend, Niyol and Nayati took their spears and set off alone.

There were many conical fish traps on the litter, stacked inside each other and woven from flexible willow. About eighteen inches in diameter at the entrance, they tapered to a smaller gap of perhaps seven or eight inches at the opposite end. Doli attached a net bag at the end, for the fish to swim into. These were big enough to hold several fish and was, Doli explained, her own variation to a more traditional trap.

Because of the number of traps, she intended to set, they would have to venture to and from the campsite several times. They tied a loop of cordage to the top and bottom of a set of traps so they could carry them on their backs, took a handful of nets and set off.

"We search for places where the water narrows but is not deep." Doli told him.

"How wide and how deep?" Yiska asked.

"Deep to my knee, narrow as there is. If it is too deep, the fish swim over the traps, too wide and they swim past."

Doli took a natural lead along the riverbank. The river itself was only about fifteen feet wide but was fast flowing, and it would be dangerous to venture into at any depth.

Yiska spotted a narrowing, by some rocks up ahead, and Doli nodded in agreement to his pointing finger. As they approached, he studied the water. The bottom was clear, and he gestured to his knee with a grin. Doli smiled back, nodded and took off her traps so she could tie a net to each one. She then carefully secured each, widthways, to a length of cordage to prevent them being taken downstream with the current. Yiska watched carefully before copying her with his.

115

"We will fish well here," Doli stated, as she picked up her traps. "Watch and do as I do!"

Stepping out into the knee-deep freezing water, she held onto a large moss-covered rock for support and laid the first trap in the water. She placed two large stones from the riverbed into the net and then two more into the cone entrance. She repeated the process with the next trap which she lay next to the first. Yiska followed her into the river, gasping as he experienced the icy temperature of the water, and laid the third of the string in the same way.

Once the traps had covered the entire width of the river, Doli picked up more stones from the riverbed and placed them on top of them, extra weight for securing them. As soon as they had finished, Yiska followed her back ashore. His feet numb from the icy water, but as she hadn't complained, neither did he!

They tied another bundle of traps and set off again. Five times they lay traps where the waters narrowed, before returning to camp.

Doli had a fire going in minutes and set some water to heat. She sat in front of it and extended her feet towards it, wriggling her toes as she did so. Yiska sat down beside her and, taking one of her feet in his hands, rubbed it She smiled and thanked him as he repeated the process with her other foot.

"I remember Niyol doing this for me when I was small. It is a good memory."

"It helps to get the circulation going," Yiska replied in a matter-of-fact manner, suddenly conscious of what he'd just done.

"The others will soon return, and they will bring fish. We will eat them tonight; eat well Yiska, the night will be cold."

Yiska nodded his agreement, and they sat close together to wait, enjoying the warmth of the fire and each other's proximity.

Niyol and Nayati returned just as the light of day disappeared. Between them they carried trout and bass, of good size.

Niyol moved to the litter and retrieved the sack of salt and some skin pouches made from carcasses of long dead deer. He filleted the fish with expert skill from a lifetime of practise before pouring salt into the pouches and alternating layers of the filleted fish with layers of salt. He lifted them carefully and laid them on the litter. Nayati handed the last four fish to Doli who skewered them, laying them on a rock by the fire to cook, next to the flat bread already baking.

During the meal, Niyol told Yiska that they would hunt again with the spears in the morning, whilst he and Doli would empty and retrieve their traps, before returning home.

Meal finished, Niyol sipped his ritual evening coffee while Doli fetched the sleeping mats from the litter and placed them close to each other by the fire. They had brought extra blankets for their night outdoors, which they soon huddled between, to combat the chilly night air.

At the first light of the pre-dawn, they set out. Niyol had given instructions to break camp at noon. Doli and Yiska set a brisk pace to the furthest set of traps from the campsite. He watched as, one by one she lifted the traps and removed the nets. She took the nets to the bank where she emptied them, removing both the fish and the debris that had collected there. Those that were still alive, she hit on the head to dispatch them, thanking the fish spirit for each offering. Then she threaded cordage through the gills and suspended them from the ends of a pole carried on the shoulder.

Yiska was soon working as hard as Doli, and after repeating this process with all of their sets, they finished with over twenty fish to carry as well as the traps and nets.

Once there, Doli gutted and filleted some fish, while Yiska loaded the traps back on the litter. She mirrored Nayati's technique for salting the fish from the night before and added them to the fillets already in the skin pouches. The rest she applied a different technique. She sliced along the bones from tail to the head on one side before turning it over and repeating the process on the other side. Then she extracted the central bones completely. The head she left untouched and once again strung them. Yiska looked at her and she explained they were for smoking, over the campfire.

"They taste other than salted fish, which is good at the end of winter."

Niyol and Nayati returned with a similar catch to the previous evening, and Doli salted them. When Niyol remarked that it was rare to experience such good fishing as this; both Nayati and Doli agreed.

Within an hour they had broken camp and were heading back to check their animal traps.

Niyol suggested that the two boys could run ahead to start on the traps, as they were so keen on running and Yiska grinned at the tease. This time though, they set off at a sensible pace and Yiska allowed Nayati to stay just in front.

As they approached, the area where the traps were, try as he could, Yiska could not spot them before Nayati; his experience was a testament to what Yiska still had to learn.

They worked in silence and had collected six traps before Nayati grunted with approval at the sight of a ground squirrel in the next. The animal was still alive and Yiska watched him dispatch it, offering thanks to the animal spirits, just as his sister had done with the fish.

Gutting the animal, he threaded it onto some sinew cordage. Then he gave it to Yiska to carry. Although Yiska knew that Nayati was making a status claim, he said nothing and carried the catch without complaint. By the time Niyol and Doli caught up with them, Yiska was carrying four squirrels and two rabbits with half their traps still to find.

As they walked higher up the mountain, it had snowed again the previous night; the temperature had fallen considerably. Their last few traps were not only empty, but completely buried in snow!

By the time they rounded the rocky outcrop that marked the boundary of their home, there was almost eight inches on the ground. It disappointed Niyol; despite the excellent success, their catch was insufficient for the entire winter, and he hoped to repeat the trip after drying and storing their catch, and a day's rest.

Chapter 18:
The Mountain Lion

After they had unloaded the litter, Niyol instructed Yiska to take care of Friend while the rest of them got to work on the meat.

Yiska led the mare away towards the small shelter, constructed for her. The structure lay fifty yards from the cave, close to a second built to store straw and hay.

This one was different though, built by Niyol many seasons ago. Established between four trees that formed a natural rectangle, he had interwoven stout willow branches driven into the ground between them on three sides, plugging gaps with spruce branches. The willow had thrived and grew foliage that completely camouflaged the shelter which now blended in with the surrounding landscape.

Inside, the shelter was draft free with the opening facing south. Friend could come and go as she pleased, but she never wandered far. The floor had a deep layer of straw, and a bundle of hay tied to one side. They stored the litter along one wall of the shelter when not in use.

Yiska spent a few minutes with the mare brushing her down with a bundle of tightly packed twigs that formed a grooming brush. He talked to her, as Niyol would, thanking her for the tireless effort she made and for the willingness with which she helped them, before setting back.

Above, the call of the eagle penetrated the silence, and he looked up. He could just see it through the treetops. It called again and again. A shiver of fear ran down his spine. Daily he saw the bird above him and had grown used to the comfort its presence brought him. They only heard it when there was danger. He searched the surrounding landscape, not knowing what he was looking for, but seeing nothing untoward.

The others! he thought starting back at a brisk pace.

As he rounded the outcrop, he stopped short at the sight before him. Niyol and Nayati stood motionless at the edge of the clearing, knives drawn. Doli was standing closer to his position with her back toward the cave entrance. They were all staring, transfixed, at a narrow, rocky ledge leading down from the mountain.

Yiska turned his head, following their gaze until his eyes alighted on a huge mountain lion, tail waving, jaws salivating, and eyes set on Doli. In her hand she held several skinned rabbits from the hunt, ready to hang and dry. The lion smelt the meat and came to investigate.

Niyol saw Yiska appear and slowly raised his hand, instructing him to remain still.

At first Yiska obeyed, his unmoving body concealing his racing thoughts. What could he do? He had no knife, no weapon of any kind, but he had to distract the lion's attention away from Doli.

The cat did not appear to have noticed his arrival. A huge male, far too intent on Doli and the meat she carried. It edged slowly towards her. Now it was close enough to see the dark markings on its muzzle, and the unusual black patch under one eye. It stalked the lower part of the ledge with consummate ease, despite being too narrow for such a large animal, it leapt down into the once-safe clearing, snarling.

High above, the eagle called out time and time again.

Suddenly, Yiska's instincts took over. He took a deep breath and ran forward, shouting and waving his arms above his head, straight towards the hungry animal. Niyol and Nayati responded moving towards the cat with their knives at the ready. The lion growled, surprised and confused, standing for a moment longer before flattening his ears, turning and rushing straight past Yiska, almost knocking him over in its haste. It then head off at a furious pace into the trees.

Yiska, adrenaline still flowing, hadn't stopped to consider his own danger as the lion had charged towards him. He raced over to Doli, enfolding her trembling body with his arms in sheer relief. He turned to Niyol, "Where did that come from?" he asked.

Niyol responded with a slow shake of his head. "I do not know. One moment it was not there, the next it was! That is often the way with animals such as these... Nayati!" he called. "Take your bow and track the beast. See that it travels far from here."

Nayati nodded and moved away, following the lion's direction.

Yiska felt the shaking in Doli's body subside and then stop and he admired the way she could take things in her stride. He released her from his embrace asking her if she was all right.

"I am well, and it pleases me you are here," she smiled warmly at him.

The old man watched their exchange and felt a warmth for the relationship he could see growing between them.

Almost as if it hadn't happened, Niyol and Doli continued with the tasks of preparing and storing the meat and fish; but Yiska, once the initial shock had worn off, relived the incident in his mind. *Did he do the right thing? What might have happened? One, perhaps more than one of them, could have been hurt!*

He trembled now, until Doli came and sat beside him, handing him a tin mug with a delicious aroma rising from it with the steam. "Drink, Yiska. I have added honey to still the after fear inside you."

Sipping at the herbal tea, he realised that she understood how he felt.

"I was so worried," he whispered. "I thought you..." his voice trailed off into silence.

"Here in the mountains, far from others, sometimes things happen. It is the way of life," she said. "It is right to thank the spirits that we are safe."

Yiska considered the rattlesnake and mountain lion and saw the truth in her words. He wondered what other adventures were to pass.

Nayati returned, as if by magic, just as they were sitting down for their evening meal.

"The lion travelled far, many miles. We are safe," he informed Niyol, who nodded, pleased with the news.

They ate the meal in silence, as was their custom but once they had finished Nayati laughed. Everybody looked at him, wondering what the joke was. He laughed so much that tears streamed down his face. Yiska looked at him in amazement. Since his arrival, he'd never heard Nayati laugh before. He couldn't stop himself from smiling.

"Nayati," Niyol said to him, "What is it that makes you laugh in this manner?"

Nayati looked straight at his grandfather and rose to his feet. "This Old Man!" he said, and ran around the cave, flailing his arms like a madman. The others, including Yiska, realised who he was mimicking, laughed with him until at last, he sat down, exhausted.

Niyol looked across at Yiska,

"It is the custom that you stand still when faced with such a hunter. It is right to make yourself seem very large, to prevent it from attacking. If you waited for a while longer, you would see Nayati and I move towards Doli, and she to us. With three together, it is not likely that the cat would attack. What you did was dangerous, and the cat may have attacked you. But it was brave!"

Then it was Nayati's turn.

"What madness made you do such a thing?"

Yiska thought carefully before responding.

"I don't understand the way of the animals, as you do, and I didn't know what to do. I thought Doli was in great danger and I had no weapon. Niyol teaches me to respect each of the creatures we share our home with, and though it threatened, I didn't wish to harm it. What I did, seemed to be the right thing to do."

"It worked this time," Niyol interrupted, before his grandson could tease Yiska more, "But if the animal was starving, it may be different."

Yiska nodded, "It would appear that I still have a lot to learn."

Doli looked at him with a little sympathy saying, "Yiska, it pleases me that you needed to protect us, for it shows you are becoming as one with us. I thank you!"

"You need to thank the eagle spirit too Doli, for it was the cry that warned me of the impending danger. I returned fast because the eagle called out so many times.

I think my spirit bird maybe yours too, for it seems only natural that each of you has a strong spirit animal to look after you."

Niyol thought about Yiska's conclusions and hoped that he was right.

"We all thank the eagle for its warning," he said.

Doli collected the plates to wash, while Niyol instructed the two boys to make a slow-burning fire outside, so that they could smoke the rest of the fish and meat. He explained to Yiska that they did this outside because of the odour. It was necessary to stay by the fire in case the cat returned.

They hung the rest of the meat in the storeroom to dry. Nayati tied some long sticks together to make two 'A' frames and then tied another between them to form the complete frame. Doli brought out the fish and meat to hang on the crosspiece and told him that by morning their food would be ready for storage.

While the meat was beginning its smoking process over the fire, Doli invited Yiska to make an ice box with her. He followed her to the side of the cave entrance where a pile of rocks lay, undisturbed for millennia and since the time of their falling from higher up the mountain. She climbed over these, pointing out a cavity lying between two large rocks, for Yiska to inspect. The cavity had deep sides, and smaller rocks lay beneath the two formed the base.

She collected snow from the ground in front of the rocks, placing it inside the gap, and then compressed it down with her glove-covered hands. She sent Yiska to fetch two stout sticks, one long and one short. When he returned, she took and used the end of the longer one to compress the snow at the bottom further, with short sharp blows.

When she had finished, Yiska could see that she'd covered the base with about six inches of ice. She collected more snow to cover the sides and repeated the process using the shorter stick until she'd covered the sides to a similar depth with ice. The rectangular box was now ready for the meat being smoked over the fire; they would fashion the lid from more compacted snow.

It would be cold that night and they agreed that they would all take turns in guarding the meat and keeping the fire going. Doli would take the first two hours, Niyol the next, followed by Nayati and Yiska. Yiska wondered what it would be like sitting in sub-zero temperatures whilst the snow fell on him and was not looking forward to the task.

When Niyol came out from the storeroom carrying a skin-covered bundle, Yiska followed with interest. Niyol unrolled it outside the cave, revealing a small tepee, large enough for one person to sit inside. He placed it, with the opening in front of the fire.

"For shelter and warmth," he explained and Yiska nodded.

Returning inside, Doli had made some pine needle tea, and they sat to drink. From the storeroom, she returned with a thick blanket slit in the centre. She gave it to Yiska and indicated that he should put his head through the hole and wear it for warmth when he was tending the fire. His shift, before first light, would be the coldest.

Then Niyol gave Yiska an object wrapped in faded buckskin. He opened it to reveal a knife which he pulled it from its leather sheath, to examine.

"It was of my brother," Niyol explained. "He made the handle from the antler of a pronghorn antelope. He no longer needs it as he walks with the spirits. After today, it is right that it becomes yours."

126

"Thank you," Yiska replied, realising the significance of the gift. "I will take great care of it."

"If I thought not, I would not burden you with the task!" Niyol told him.

Nayati's eyes flashed with jealous anger as he felt Niyol should have passed such a treasure on to him.

Starting her shift Doli went outside while the others settled on their sleeping mats by the fire to rest. Nayati woke Yiska in the early hours of the morning.

"After one hour, take the meat from the frame for it to cool," he instructed, then lay down on his sleeping mat, his eyes closing instantly.

Yiska put on the blanket that Doli had given him and disappeared outside. It was snowing heavily, and the stiffening breeze accentuated the bitter cold. He felt the chill and took shelter in the tepee. It provided excellent cover, and it trapped warmth from the fire within. The mesmerising flames soon relaxed him, and he forgot about the cold as he thought about the time he had spent with this family and how close he had become to each of them. Each of them except Nayati.

He wanted so much to be friends with him but Nayati rejected his efforts at every level. He'd endured ridicule and scorn for a long time now and even as he thought about it anger grew inside. What else could he do to prove himself worthy? There was no obvious answer to the question, and he didn't know what to do about him. He kicked out in frustration and anger at the rocks around the fire sending a bouquet of sparks skyward.

When the time had passed, he removed the meat and placed it to cool on the snow, which was now about a foot deep on the clearing, except near the fire. He wondered how much more would fall during the winter months. It will be deep, he thought, if this is anything to go by!

As the darkness lightened, Doli emerged from the cave; she too clad in a blanket like his, to collect the meat. He followed her to the icebox; and watched as she once more compressed the fresh snow, fallen into it during the night. She placed the meat inside, covering each fillet with fresh snow; then collected more snow to lie on top. This too she compacted down until it was solid and buried at least six inches deep.

The snow fell for the next three days without respite until it was about two feet deep. Visibility was down to just a few yards, so apart from clearing the entrance, they did not venture outside the cave.

Chapter 19:
Who am I?

The young boy glanced around the room to check he was alone. It was large and contained eight identical beds. Each had a cupboard beside it with three small drawers and a hanging space for clothes. The top drawer was lockable.

Checking the room was empty for the third time, he removed the key, he wore around his neck on a piece of string and inserted it into the lock. He twisted it and heard the click as it released. Withdrawing the key, he returned it to its place of concealment and opened the drawer. Inside was a single object, a box, which he took it out.

The box was eight inches long, four inches wide and three deep. Made of wood, it had a gold-coloured inlay, two double lines, that travelled around the perimeter of the lid. The boy hugged the box close to his chest before laying it down on the iron-framed bed, covered in a military grey blanket. He raised the lid and emptied the contents onto the blanket.

The first item he picked up was a silver St. Christopher medallion on a silver chain. In terms of monetary value, it was not worth much, but the boy held it as if it had come from a vault in Fort Knox. After checking to see that he was still alone, he slipped the chain over his head.

Next were three photographs; one showed a tall, slim, handsome Indian, dressed in denims and a checked shirt. The second was of a woman; shorter, with long dark hair. She had a soft, pleasant looking face that the boy thought was beautiful, and tears formed in his eyes as he gazed at her. The last photograph featured them at a ceremony. The man in a dark suit, the woman in a long, flowing, ivory coloured dress.

Underneath the pictures were two medals attached to short coloured ribbons, the metal starting to dull. Although he didn't know what they were, they seemed important. He lay them to one side and reached out for the box once more.

Pulling at the fabric lining at the bottom, he lifted it away from the side of the box and inserted his finger and thumb in the gap; withdrawing an envelope concealed within. Inside the envelope, he withdrew a single sheet of paper. He stared in wonder at the beautiful italic writing flowing across the page; but its contents were to remain a mystery as he couldn't read the words. With a smile in his mind, he placed all the objects back in the box, returned it to the drawer and locked it.

Yiska opened his eyes realising something was wrong. He lay on the floor of the cave, near to the storeroom entrance. Looking up, he saw Doli's beautiful, concerned face looking down at him.

"What?" he started.

"Be still Yiska," she commanded. "Drink!" Yiska drank from the cup she offered, aware of an acute pain at the front of his head.

"What happened?" he asked, grimacing at the pain that throbbed like a drum.

"You fell down. One moment you fetched wood from the store and then you were on the floor."

Niyol appeared by Doli with a damp cloth which he placed on Yiska's forehead.

"Is there pain?" he asked and Yiska nodded, wishing he hadn't as it seared his forehead.

He pointed to the front of his head and Niyol moved away to make one of his herbal teas. Doli helped him to sit up.

"You must return to the fire," she suggested, and then added "You worried me!"

As he stood, the pain became intense, and he could not help clasping his hand to his forehead. Yiska saw the worry on Doli's face and removed his hand despite the pain.

"It's all right, it's just a headache!" he told her.

She said nothing but helped him to his sleeping mat, pushing him down gently, so that he lay on his back. Yiska said nothing, directing a small smile of thanks towards her.

They let him rest for a while and Yiska felt the pain slowly subsiding. Niyol brought the tea for him to drink. Again, Yiska asked what had happened.

Niyol repeated the explanation that Doli had given, then asked, "Were you with the spirits?"

"I don't know for sure, Teacher, but there were images, powerful images, clear and detailed. I don't know what they mean, but it was me I was seeing."

Niyol nodded with a frown of concentration. "Maybe the spirits are returning your memories. Later, you can tell us what you saw, but first you must rest. How is the pain?"

"The pain is becoming less," Yiska told him, "I want to know what these images mean."

"It will be as you ask Yiska but rest now."

So Yiska closed his eyes and did as instructed. Doli sat close to him and took his hand in hers.

He did not wake until late the following morning. Nayati looked at him with disgust.

"You sleep as long as a baby, Yiska. How is it that when the snow stops and there is work, you sleep longer?" he enquired, but there was no real scorn in his voice, and he hid his relief that Yiska appeared to be all right.

"I'm not concerned about the work, since I'm quicker to complete the tasks," Yiska replied, grinning.

Nayati scowled and went outside as Doli walked towards him.

"You are better for your sleep?" she asked.

Yiska nodded. "Will you walk with me for a while?" he asked.

She smiled, pleased that he'd asked her. They put their blankets over their heads and moved outside into their snow-covered world.

Yiska blinked at the brightness of the light outside. Covered now with at least three feet of pure snow, everything looked pristine. The sky was a beautiful shade of deep blue and the sun glistened off the surface of the snow, making it sparkle like early morning dew drops. The icy temperature made them catch their breath though. Yiska grinned.

"It is beautiful," he stated the obvious, not out of necessity but because it demanded him to.

They stumbled towards the cliff edge to observe the view below, laughing as their feet sunk deep into the snow. The scene was stunning.

The trees sagged under the weight of the snow on their branches. It covered every tiny finger on each branch. Accustomed to seeing the greenery which had disappeared completely, the scene resembled an Antarctic desert; wild, desolate and peaceful.

"I want to see the forest," Yiska told her.

Doli nodded, and they walked towards the rocky outcrop and rounded the bend. Yiska realized the penetrating silence as they entered. The trees were heavy with snow but there was less underfoot than by the cave. They walked about for several minutes, before Doli said it was time to go back to tend to their chores. As they passed underneath a large conifer, a branch emptied its load onto Doli's head. Yiska laughed as he brushed it off of her. Doli laughed too and took a handful of snow and thrusting it down Yiska's neck in retaliation for his laughter.

"This is fun, yes?" she asked, with raised eyebrows.

Niyol looked up as they came back. He had watched the bond between them develop and strengthen over the past weeks, just as the bond had developed between himself and the boy. They are at one with each other; he thought. It would please me if Nayati made the same effort with Yiska that Yiska makes with him.

Niyol beckoned them towards him and called Nayati over.

"The snow has stopped, we must use this time," he told them. "Nayati and Yiska you will cut and bring more wood to the store. Doli you will attend to the needs of Friend. I will prepare shafts for arrows, for we must hunt to add to our food stocks."

Soon hard at work, Nayati and Yiska took turns to cut while the other collected the cut pieces, making it an unspoken competition to see who could cut more wood. Nayati was more adept with the axe, and Yiska had to make more trips back to the cave with the cut wood.

Doli finished her task first and returned to the cave to clean. She took outside, and beat, the sleeping mats and blankets before choosing some salted fish to make a broth for their evening meal. They would need to eat well to replenish the physical energy they'd spent at work during the day and keeping warm in the low temperatures.

After eating, Niyol asked Yiska to tell them about the visions he'd seen the day before, which he did, telling him about the room in great detail. When Niyol said nothing, he continued describing the box and the objects it contained.

"I will give this thought before I tell you what they might mean," Niyol told Yiska.

Although disappointed, Yiska understood that Niyol would say nothing without due consideration.

Doli asked Yiska to describe the man and woman in the photograph and he surprised her with the level of detail.

"Did you know them?" she asked.

"In the vision I'm sure I did, but as I talk to you now, I don't know them at all," he replied.

"What about the St Christopher?" she asked, "what is it?"

Yiska explained that St. Christopher was the patron saint of travellers.

"And the medals?" she enquired.

"The medals are from a war, but what they mean, or which war they are from, I don't know," he told her.

"It is a strange group of things," she said, "They do not seem to belong together, but are of great concern to the boy in your vision."

"Yiska! I am understanding of this," said Doli suddenly. "If I journey away from Niyol and Nayati, I would take of each of them and I would not be alone, I would take of yours too," she added.

Yiska nodded in agreement.

Niyol looked at Yiska and then said. "I am sure these visions are because the spirits release some of your memories. The man was Indian, and the woman from the western world; you are of mixed spirits. My thought is that these may be your parents. The St. Christopher, a gift from her to you, the medals might be your father's or his fathers. There have been many wars. Men earn these in battle for a brave act. These things belonged to you."

He paused and drank some of his tea.

"And the room?" Yiska asked.

"It is my thought that you lived in a place for many children. There is a name, but I do not know it," Niyol continued.

"An orphanage," Yiska said, "You mean an orphanage."

Niyol nodded.

"If this is the case, my parents either left me there from choice or circumstances, something happened to them," Yiska said, in a quiet voice.

"We cannot guess at the reasons, Yiska, for to do so will leave conflict in your mind. The spirits returned memories; it is my thinking that more will return. Someone beat you close to death. The spirits protect you from the past until your strength returns. You must wait; the memories will return," Niyol finished.

"You must have many questions that need answers," Doli suggested.

Yiska nodded. "It's true, there are many; but I'll try to be patient as Niyol suggests."

135

Chapter 20:
The Snowstorm

For the next few days it snowed without stopping and temperatures plummeted. The sun, in a sudden state of hibernation, remained hidden and declined to offer its comforting embrace to man or creature. After the fifth day it made a brief appearance and tempted the family from their cave. Even this early in the year it emitted a glow of warmth, obscuring the bitter cold from their thoughts.

Niyol walked away to find Friend, encouraging her gently to brave the elements and exercise. He brushed her down and cleaned out her home before finishing his tasks by giving the mare fresh hay.

Nayati had set off to fetch more wood from the outside store. It was amazing how much wood the fire they kept constantly burning used, but being shut inside for the past four days, their internal supply had run low. He had refused Yiska's offer of help, having endured far more of his presence than he'd wanted too already. He still wrestled with his feelings about Yiska, the torment inside his head, and the long period of internment in the cave, had left him irritable and short-tempered. Time out could only benefit him.

Yiska and Doli, understood Nayati's need for space and took advantage of the lull in the snow to go for a walk. Their happiness at being alone together again, obvious by the smiles of contentment they carried.

Twenty yards from the cave Doli took hold of Yiska's hand and interlocked their fingers. Surprised and pleased by her initiative Yiska looked down into the eyes that were already seeking his. Something tugged deep inside, and he realised his desperate need of her presence. He smiled trying to hide the feelings that coursed through him in case she read what he was experiencing and pulled away.

She returned the smile with her full radiance, brighter than the sun itself and bringing a warmth that far outweighed its own meagre attempt. Doli experienced the pull too and turned her face away just as it started to flush, and the two of them fell into step and just enjoyed being together.

An hour and a half later, and deep into the forest, they'd failed to notice the sun's disappearance, and the forming, and lowering of a cloud mass that now enveloped the entire sky. The temperature dropped and Doli suddenly shivered bringing awareness that something was amiss to the forefront.

"Yiska we must leave! The snow will return soon; it will be heavy, and we will not see where we travel."

"What do you mean by that?" Yiska asked, sensing her alarm.

"The land, the sky and the air will be as one, white, everything will disappear. The trails too. We have journeyed too far, and the others do not know the way we travel."

Yiska gripped her hand tighter and turned to face the direction they'd come from. He took a step and pulled at her hand and they started back. Moments later the snow fell, large, voluminous flakes. The intensity of it surprised Yiska as it concealed the canopy above them. A stiff breeze arrived, snapping at their faces and forcing the vertical falling flakes into an almost horizontal flight. It increased and drove the snow harder; the world became an opaque bath of milky whiteness and all substance vanished.

"Yiska, we must dig into the snow to shelter from this." Her voice with a vibrato quality emphasised her need to escape the cold.

"I saw an incline just ahead of us before we lost our vision. It had a heavy drift of snow against it. It would be the perfect spot for what you're suggesting. Keep with me Doli and don't let go for anything."

They stumbled forward against the still increasing force of the wind. Twice they walked into the trunk of a tree until Yiska started up the incline. He remembered it ascend for about twenty feet and he continued forward until he estimated that they were about halfway up. The wind whipped through the trees above, howling in protest. Yiska dropped to his knees and pulled Doli down too.

"Dig!" he commanded, and the two of them scooped away swathes of loose snow not yet frozen solid.

Soon a cave like hole took shape and Doli shouted instructions to dig wider inside the hole but not to disturb the entrance. This time Yiska followed her instructions and made the inside larger whilst she firmed up and closed down the entrance. The hole, now just big enough for them to squeeze through, was much larger inside and Yiska pushed Doli in first and followed. Both of them shivered violently and their hands were numb with the cold of digging out the snow.

Yiska grabbed hers and blew on them. After a minute or two it had an effect and she couldn't prevent gasping at the pain as life returned in her fingers. She gave the same treatment to Yiska's hands. He placed his arm around her and pulled her close trying to share what body heat they had but already the cold had permeated deep into their core and neither could prevent their shivers.

"Take off your buckskins," Yiska ordered her. Even though he knew what they had to do, he couldn't hide the embarrassment at making such a demand.

She noticed his colouring change and came to his rescue.

"It is good that you know the ways of survival Yiska. We will make a mattress with them to protect us from the cold beneath us. Our ponchos will be as blankets."

"I'm glad that you know about these things too." Yiska replied, unable to hide his relief.

Though cramped, they both removed their buckskins and manipulated them into position without leaving their makeshift cave. They then removed their ponchos and draped them over. Yiska stretched out and told Doli to lie against him. He wrapped his arms around her, and they lay in silence. Their bodies warmed, and the shivering subsided. Yiska turned to face her and Doli altered her position to match and keep her body tight against his.

"An hour ago, the sun was shining, and we were walking without a worry and now we could be here for days. I am sorry Doli, you would be safe at home if I hadn't suggested the walk Doli. It will worry the others."

"Do not think in this way Yiska. I wanted to be with you. We will return home when the snow stops. Nayati and Grandfather know I have the ways to survive, they know also that I am with you and that it is easier to survive when there are two."

"You have a way of making everybody feel good about themselves Doli. You are always so considerate; I am glad that I have you in my life."

"It is good that you think this, but you are kind also Yiska. You do things for everyone without complaint, even Nayati who is not good to you. It is a matter to discuss with him."

"He sees me as a threat to your existence here in the forest, I understand why, and in some ways, I respect that. I want him to be my friend, but I want to be his too. He is a good person I know, and I will wear him down by being myself and not through confrontation."

"It will be hard; he is as one with his ways."

"I know, but I can be stubborn too, I will not give up my hopes."

"Grandfather says that you will challenge each other in ways that will make you both stronger and better as soon as Nayati sees you for who you are. He does not deserve to have you as a friend until he sees you as I do."

"How do you see me Doli?"

She averted her eyes and there was a pause before she answered.

"I have not the words to answer that question."

"How do you see me Yiska?"

Yiska didn't answer. He kept his eyes locked with hers and leaned forward placing his lips against hers.

She made no move to pull away and when at last their lips parted, he said.

"I do not have the words either," and pulled her tighter to him, drinking the scent of her body.

Six hours passed before the snow abated and already it was dark outside their hole. They'd checked the outside conditions several times during that period and both of them were secretly pleased that they needed to stay where they were. This time several stars were visible

140

through the canopy. Time to move before the snow returned.

"Shouldn't we wait until morning; we could get lost travelling in the dark?"

"It is not as dark as nights without snow. The forest here I know; we will be at the cave before the light of the morning."

"Are you sure?" Yiska asked and despite his best attempt could not hide his disappointment at having to leave.

Doli suddenly realised why he suddenly sounded morose.

"We will make other times to be alone together Yiska, but we must go."

"Was I that obvious?"

Doli smiled. "There is one thing that I would ask of you before we leave Yiska."

"What is it?"

"Would you touch my lips with yours as before?"

Yiska lowered his head and their lips caressed. He held them there, engulfing her in his arms, pulling her closer, locking her in.

They looked flushed and happy when they broke apart.

"Is there a name for this touching?"

"It's called kissing!" Yiska answered surprised.

"I have little knowledge of this and yet I remember my father touching me with his lips on my head," Doli said, before adding. "You are the first to show me this with the lips," she smiled, and then added, "it is good."

"Didn't your mother ever kiss you?"

"I have memories of my mother, none of kissing."

"It is a sign of affection between two people."

"I understand but have little knowledge of this."

Yiska let the comment go with a nod of understanding and they walked. Four hours later they reached the safety of the cave. Niyol and Nayati appeared asleep and Yiska realised how confident they each were in their shared knowledge and abilities. Doli moved her sleeping mat closer to Yiska's, and they settled down to sleep. She reached out her hand in search of his, found it and interlocked their fingers. As soon as they lay still Niyol raised an eyelid and cast a gaze upon them. He noticed the new positions of their sleeping mats and connection of their hands; something had happened, he was sure, and he would talk to Doli about it later. He closed his eyes and all in the cave was silent but for the steady breathing of its inhabitants.

Chapter 21:
Shattered Peace

Doli and Yiska slept in later than usual after the night's adventure. Nayati wanted to wake Doli up so that she would attend her normal morning duties, making breakfast and a warm tea for them all. He wouldn't entertain doing the tasks for himself, this was woman's work, and when Niyol prevented him from waking her he left the cave in a disgruntled fashion.

Niyol smiled and made a mental note to educate his grandson on the ways of the western world.

It was likely that, in the next few years, they would leave the cave to seek adventure in the wider world. For so long now, he had adopted the Navajo lifestyle that he cursed himself for leaving it for so long. Nayati, in particular, would find it difficult adapting to western ways, such was his strength of conviction about living as a Navajo.

He also wanted to educate him about being of mixed spirits and what it was like on both the Indian reservation and in the western world where prejudice and racial tension was commonplace in both societies. Nayati had already tasted that after the trading market.

Niyol took on Doli's duties and found pleasure in preparing his granddaughters breakfast and early morning tea. So much of what she did for him, and her brother was unappreciated and yet she took her duties without complaint or need for them to recognize her hard work. As soon as she stirred and sat up, he passed her some tea.

"It is good when you make me tea Old Man," she said, smiling at his efforts.

"As it is for me each day I wake in this place." He replied returning the smile. "You were home late; it is my thinking that you looked after Yiska and showed him our ways in such conditions?"

"I did not need to show him of our ways for he had knowledge of this. He cared after me."

"It is good that he has this understanding but tell me how was it not to take charge."

"It was strange, but Yiska was acting in the right way. He made a shelter in the snow. We teach him many things, and he has been respectful in learning them. It is right for him to teach us his ways also."

"Is it right to learn his ways or stay with the ways of our ancestors?"

"He has knowledge of things we do not. A wise old man told me we learn what we need by watching and listening to all things. If this is the way of the Dineh, we will learn from Yiska if we listen and watch him."

"The Old Man gave you excellent advice." Niyol stated, at her memory of his teachings.

"Yiska showed me how he is. The storm of snow was bad, I have no memory of one that was worse. He was strong, and careful, he cared only for me, he did not think of himself. We build the snow shelter and my hands were of no further use; I had no life in them. Yiska blew on them and rubbed until the life returned."

144

Yiska stirred and sat up, ending the conversation between Niyol and Doli. Niyol passed him a tea.

"You are rested Yiska?"

"Yes! Thank you, we had quite an adventure last night."

"I learned of what happened. You are wise in the poor conditions and thought only of your companion. I am pleased for your ways Yiska."

"It's easy to care for Doli in the same way that she cares for us each day."

"You are right in what you say, and it is good you have knowledge of how to act in such conditions. Knowledge is for survival in places like this."

"Doli worked until she lost the feeling in her hands and her body temperature dropped to where she couldn't stop shivering. She is strong and brave Niyol." Yiska added, before reaching out and placing his hand on her arm.

He squeezed it gently and smiled at her.

Niyol noticed the smile. In Yiska's eyes, there was more than affection. Doli returned the smile with her own and Niyol witnessed the same closeness between them. They are becoming one with each other and he remembered how it had been when he'd first exchanged such feelings with his late wife. How he wished to see that smile from her again, in reality, instead of in his dreams.

Nayati entered the cave and saw Yiska's hand on his sister's arm. He walked over and wrenched it away from Doli, gripping it like a vice, making no attempt to release it.

"Why do you dishonour our ways by touching her in this way? I forbid it, you are not family," he shouted, and Yiska saw the venom in his eyes.

Nayati was close to losing any sense of control, he knew it.

He replied in his typical quiet, reserved manner. "I do not dishonour your ways or your sister. If you had heard what I said you would understand this. Now release my arm."

Nayati gripped it harder. "Everything you do here is not real. You are not a Navajo and you will never be one. You are like those who are not Navajo, you respect nothing, people, land, creatures, life."

"How can you know what I am like Nayati you are not interested in knowing me? You are no more Navajo than I am. You don't respect me, and you don't respect Doli. Now for the last time release my arm."

Niyol noticed the change in Yiska's tone, Nayati was pushing too hard.

Doli spoke up trying to diffuse the tension. "Nayati, Yiska saved me from losing my hands to the black sickness, that steals the fingers. He built a snow shelter, kept me warm with his body and cared for me in the ways that you would have."

Instead of having the desired effect she had hoped for, it enraged him further.

"You laid with him and shared the warmth of his body. This is not the way of our people; he is not the only one to dishonour our ways; you did also."

His voice was now so intimidating that Niyol wanted to intervene and yet something nagged at him to keep silent and watch how this developed. Confrontation was inevitable between the two of them despite Yiska's constant avoidance tactics. It might be the only thing that might end it.

"Do not speak to me about dishonour Nayati because you show it towards me and your sister all the time. Don't you dare accuse her of dishonour because nothing is further from the truth."

Niyol saw a fire of anger in Yiska eyes.

146

"I have asked you twice and I will not ask you again," Yiska said, staring hard into Nayati's eyes.

He placed his hand on top of Nayati's and bent his fingers backwards. Nayati applied even more pressure and the immediate area around his grip turned white. No matter how hard he tried, he could not prevent Yiska bending back his fingers almost to the point of breaking them. Both of them concentrated until just before his fingers broke when he suddenly released them with a scowl of pain and anger.

With lightning speed Yiska drew back his arm and launched a clenched fist at Nayati's jaw. It connected where he had aimed and Nayati flew backward into a heap on the ground.

"Yiska take this outside!" Niyol commanded and held Doli back from intervening.

"This must happen if there is to be peace here."

Tears flowed down Doli's cheeks as Yiska moved aside the entrance blanket and ducked through the entrance.

"I wait for you outside Navajo man," he taunted the still prone Nayati.

Nayati almost jumped up in his haste to follow Yiska out. He found him waiting calmly, hands to his sides. Niyol and Doli followed him out.

"I only wanted to be your friend Nayati, but you won't even give me a chance, where's the honour in that?"

"You are not worthy of being my friend, you are hopeless in the ways of my people, you like doing women's work. Where is the warrior in you?"

"The warrior is here, look in front of you and see it for the first time. I am the one who put you on the ground. Where is the warrior in you?"

Nayati bellowed and charged at Yiska who waited until the last millisecond before sidestepping and giving Nayati a shove. He lost his balance and sprawled to the floor.

"You seem to like the ground Nayati. Are you enjoying the dishonour I now show you, the endless ridicule and scorn, do you like that too? Why don't you get up and try to hit me? You want to hit me, don't you? Stop fighting like a woman."

Again, Nayati yelled in rage and charged at Yiska. Feinting left and right, he tried to offset any move that Yiska might make and then as he was about to smother him in a bear hug and bring him down, Yiska vanished. He had dropped onto his back before Nayati connected. Raising a leg, he placed his foot on Nayati's chest and propelled him upward and forward. Nayati landed several feet away in deep snow which prevented him having the wind knocked from his lungs.

"You do seem to like the ground here Nayati, maybe you should bring your sleeping mat out here tonight. Tell you what, I'll make this easy for you, attack me again and I promise I won't move from the spot. Come on, even a child could hit a stationary target. Perhaps I should kneel for you that would make it easy for you."

Nayati rose to his feet once more. Doli cried out and tried to move between them. Again, Niyol stopped her.

"They must sort this out, it is the only way."

"Yiska will get hurt."

"Worry for Nayati for Yiska has skills that Nayati does not and he can control his anger. I am not liking this confrontation but Nayati needs to learn a lesson."

Doli refrained from saying anything else but the tears continued to flow.

Nayati approached Yiska once more, slowly this time, and Yiska kept his feet planted where they were.

"Come on Nayati, hit me, this is what you want."

Nayati swung his fist towards Yiska's face but missed. Yiska had leant to the side but had kept his feet still. He countered with a jab that split Nayati's lip. Nayati grunted and backed off.

"Is that it Nayati have we finished; can I get breakfast? Since you can't seem to hit me this is getting rather pointless don't you think?"

Nayati came in again but his swing was slow and telegraphed and Yiska hit him hard in the stomach. Nayati fell coughing and fighting to regain his breath. Yiska moved over him.

"I want you to understand Nayati, that the race we had in the forest. I could have won that, and I spared you the defeat and allowed you to hold your head up high. But you! You have never given me the slightest consideration. Even now I like you Nayati, I want to be as good as you at the things you do, I want to be your friend. You only want to drive me away.

"Guess what Nayati, I'm not going anywhere, I like it here, being with all of you, including you. But this, the way you treat me stops now, I've had enough of it! If it doesn't, I will pay you in kind three times for every once you ridicule you me. But I won't do it here, I'll save it for the trade markets where you can experience the real hurt. Whatever your problems with me are, get over it and start afresh and I will not hold a grudge with you."

Nayati struggled to his feet once more. His movements were slow and predictable and Yiska saw it coming. The fist launched and Yiska blocked it with his left arm. He let go with a right uppercut that snapped Nayati's head backwards. Nayati fell motionless.

The anger left Yiska; his shoulders slumped, and his eyes filled with moisture that fell.

"I am sorry Nayati, why can't you like me like I do you? His voice, only a whisper, carried to Niyol."

The old man moved forward.

"Do not trouble yourself over what happened here. Nayati needed to learn a lesson, about how to treat others but also about misjudging an opponent. Even in battle you show restraint. It is my thinking that in the place where you grew up fighting was necessary to survive. You have skills in this and perhaps there will be a time when you will teach Nayati."

"I am sorry Niyol, I didn't want this to happen."

"I have seen for long enough how you have searched for other ways to end the problems between you and Nayati."

High above the eagle screeched, repeatedly.

"It would seem as if I have annoyed the spirits." Yiska said as they all looked upward.

Yiska knelt down and placed his hands under Nayati's body. He lifted him into his arms and stood up walking to the cave entrance and ducked low. Inside, he lay him down gently on his sleeping mat and fetched a cloth and water. Gently, he wiped away the blood from Nayati's nose and washed the rest of his face. He lay a blanket over him.

"One day you will be my friend Nayati."

Doli watched all this from inside the doorway, he hadn't heard her come in. She moved towards him.

"I will tend my brother Yiska."

Yiska avoided eye contact. He couldn't speak. He stood and headed toward the doorway.

"Yiska," she called

He straightened, paused for a few seconds, and left without turning.

150

Chapter 22:
Shame

Niyol watched Yiska emerge from the cave and saw the anguish still etched in his face. His pale eyes were moistening again and Niyol knew the boy needed to vent the powerful emotions coursing through his mind. He followed him, wanting to be there for him, when he was ready.

The old man had seen many forms of physical violence in his time, but it was rare to see someone show such restraint during the heat of the fight. Yiska had not wanted this, only Nayati's dishonour of Doli had forced the reaction.

It wasn't just the fight either. For weeks Yiska had endured ridicule and scorn from Nayati. Endured it all without complaint; in truth, it goaded him to try harder at everything he did. Again, he wouldn't have fought today if it hadn't of involved Doli. His thoughts raced as he walked.

What about the developing relationship between him and Doli? Doli had feelings for him, she wore her heart for everybody to see, but Yiska? They knew nothing of his past although there was plenty to like and even admire.

Niyol's beliefs told him a man's past shaped and directed his future. Yiska had a troubled past; he was sure, a victim of some of abuse, but he could take care of himself. In his past he'd learned to fight. A man only fights when there is either the need for it or for the enjoyment of it, and Yiska had not enjoyed fighting, so he'd learnt for need. Most likely for his own protection. Considering the condition he was in when he first found him, and his competent skill at fighting, more than one person had beaten him.

Another thought crossed Niyol's mind. Yiska's hands, his knuckles, there had been no wounds there. Either he hadn't fought off his attackers, or he'd become unconscious quickly and beaten whilst down.

The old man walked on until he stopped at a sound ahead. He looked upwards and made out the eagle between gaps in the trees, it circled ahead of his position. Surely, his belief in Yiska was right, the constant presence of the eagle verified it. He was here to do good, why else would he have such a powerful spirit guide?

As he edged forward the noise grew louder, and he recognised the sound of a sob followed by a spoken plea asking why. Yiska suddenly came into view as Niyol rounded a tree. He was kneeling down in a small snow-covered clearing facing up toward the eagle. Niyol retreated a few yards.

The boy was talking to the eagle and to Niyol's surprise it answered with its customary screech. Prior to this, it called only when there was danger present. Niyol sensed no such danger and decided not to interrupt, showing respect to both the boy and creature.

For an hour Yiska called out to the noble bird and Niyol heard it answer. The directness of communication shocked him. It had always been his belief that spirit totems only left signs. His belief that Yiska was here for a purpose grew, he was a good person–no matter of his past–here to follow a trail set by the spirits themselves.

The communication ceased, and all became silent. Niyol moved forward and entered the clearing.

"I seek the boy I found in the desert. I wish that he follows still the trail of recovery in both body and mind."

"You already know that my body has healed Old Man."

"And what of the mind?"

"The mind is full of doubt that I can control my actions, full of doubt that I'm a good person and full of guilt at what I did to Nayati. It is full of regret at the pain I have caused Doli and full of the dishonour that I have shown you by what I did to your grandson."

Niyol felt for the boy, even now he was blaming himself for everything that had happened although it wasn't the case.

"A man must judge his actions by deciding if what he has done is right. Whatever the answer is he will ask the same question of himself again at what he does next. In this manner he will journey through life seeking always to do what is right. The spirits are there to guide. Listen to them for they teach us lessons about the past, the now and the future. It is not always clear which time the lessons are for. It is for you to discover. In this way you honour the spirits by thinking about what they teach. You have spoken to the spirits?" Niyol asked, already knowing the answer.

"I have spoken to the eagle as you would do, it has not answered my questions."

"Did it answer at all?"

"Not in reply to my questions."

"It is the way of the spirits. When the spirit speaks you must listen. Do not expect answers that are clear. When it speaks it likes or does not like what you say. It is your choice to make this clear. It does not answer questions for it knows that the way of good is by thinking. What you do must happen after what you think. In this way it should be right." Niyol paused. "There is much to think about."

Niyol saw a flash of hope in the boy's face before it disappeared, replaced with fear and apprehension.

"Niyol I think I was a bad person in the past."

"Why do you think this?"

"Someone beat me and left me for dead, I can fight, and most of all, I know this deep inside."

"Is it a feeling Yiska or is it the fear of not knowing?"

"I can't tell."

"Listen to me and listen well Yiska. I am not a spirit guide, but I have lived for a long time and have learned much. I have watched you since I brought you here and bringing you to my home was right. This is what I think about your fears."

Yiska met Niyol's eyes and again the flash of hope passed across them.

"You have shown that you are a good person by what you do and what you say. Nayati has challenged you from the first moment you came. You answer with respect although, but this is difficult. This trouble between you and Nayati causes Doli more pain than the fight. You have not disappointed her by how you acted today because it was clear that this would happen."

"And what about the dishonour I have shown you?"

"There has been no dishonour to me. I have taught Nayati much of what he knows but I cannot teach him how to feel. He is not wrong in the way he feels, no man chooses how to feel, but he is wrong in how he shows it. In the Navajo language Nayati means one who wrestles.

He wrestles to live in the true way of a Navajo instead of being of his years. Nayati has forgotten how to be young.

"In life you learn lessons from all. Our ways are sheltered in the mountains. Nayati has little knowledge of the ways of the outside world except the memories of a small boy. He needs other than me to learn from; you are the first. It is hard to learn from others of your own age when you are young. He is learning from you, but he does not recognise this. You cause him to question himself and he does not always like the answers."

"He will like me even less now."

"For a while it will be so but if he opens his heart, he will understand he has always liked you."

"Should I speak to Doli about this?"

"You have feelings for her that is not as a sister."

The shock of the statement made Yiska's eyes open wider. He believed he'd concealed his feelings from the others because of the possibility of breaking any Navajo custom he was unaware of; the last thing he wanted to do was to disrespect their culture and beliefs.

"How do you know this?"

"It is clear. There was a woman, I loved more than life itself. I journey to be with her each year. It is not the only reason for the journey. It is against the way of our people, for in truth the Navajo fear death and celebrate life.

"I lived in the outside world for a while with my wife and we learned of their ways. Many people who lose someone they love, visit their last places of rest and talk to those who have departed. I find comfort in doing the same.

"Nayati is correct, it is not the way of the Dineh to show liking between man and woman by touching.

"Doli has no experience of such matters, she has seen no others to learn how to behave. Each of you have mixed spirits and I have been wrong to teach only of one way.

"I cannot tell you how to love her for you know how already. It is the way that people are born with this knowledge. What you do now, you must work out together. I am here if you need my help."

"Thank you, Teacher."

"It is time to return now, I am in need for some of Doli's rabbit stew and pine needle tea."

Chapter 23:
Rage

Nayati regained consciousness just after Yiska left the cave. His eyes fell upon those of his sisters and he turned away as the anger, returned.

"Do not look upon me sister for the shame I feel from your actions is more than I can bear right now."

"Do not talk to me of shame Nayati and do not speak of my actions."

"My sister acts in ways against the customs of our people."

"And who is it that acts in the ways of people with problems of the mind? You show no respect to Yiska and treat him less than human for all the time he has shared our home. This is the way of a boy who acts bad for not having his own way. You show no respect for me. Yiska saved me from the black sickness and you did not question how I am. Instead, you rage because he put his hand on my arm.

"This is of his knowing, not Navajo, but not wrong in his eyes. It is so, that you should talk to him of this matter. as our grandfather does, but no, you act like a baby. It is I who can no longer look at you."

With that said Doli left the stunned Nayati where he lay and left the cave.

The rage inside increased at the way she had spoken to him and he got to his feet. He went into his private space and took out a pair of blankets, extra clothing and essentials like tinder and his own medicine pouch. Going outside he uncovered some frozen food and packed that too. Doli returned just as he finished.

"I am leaving. I will return when I am ready. You will tell the Old Man?"

"I will tell him. Nayati, come back with peace in your heart." Doli implored.

Nayati didn't answer, he just turned, walked away, rounded the bend and disappeared into the forest.

A few minutes after, Yiska and Niyol appeared. They listened carefully to what she told them before Yiska suggested that he went after him and brought him back.

"There are times when a man must be alone with his thoughts and this is so for Nayati. Always, he is this way, when trouble cause doubts in his mind. The knowledge to survive is his, even when the winter is at its worst. We will respect his need for he will be safe."

"The anger is much in him Grandfather."

"The walking and the cold will help drive this away." Niyol replied. "Time alone is what he needs. He will find his path after thinking."

"I hope he does." Yiska added.

"It is the way of things."

"Doli you and I should talk." Yiska suggested, but averted eye contact.

"It will be so, but not now." Doli answered, she too avoided eye contact.

Niyol intervened. "Waiting allows time for thought before talk, make what you say more right."

Yiska remained feeling morose, made even worse now by Nayati's decision to leave. It seemed as if his actions had forced the issue and now, he had driven Nayati away.

He desperately wanted to talk to Doli, but she had been emphatic about waiting, reinforced by Niyol too. They were probably right, but he needed to quell all the concerns in his mind now, it was torture and Niyol's words of wisdom weren't enough. Doli also had the gift of being able to listen, just as her Grandfather but her responses to things he said were much more direct, poignant and immediate where Niyol would often finish with an unanswered question.

Wondering what to do, he too left the cave and went for a walk. With a clear sky, there was no imminent threat of snow to be seen and he retraced the path he and Nayati had raced, where they had shared a few moments of something different from the distance that was more commonplace between them.

After half an hour he sat on the fallen tree that marked the end of the course and resurrected the entire race from his memory. He remembered the words they had taunted each other with and the pleasure they had experienced from the exchange. The smile it evoked left his face quickly as he recalled how Nayati had withdrawn back into his pre-race attitude immediately after. He wondered what would have happened if he had edged Nayati out and won the race, but it was too late now, what was done was done.

The eagle still circled above him and he realised how important the bird had become, not just as a guard or protector. It was so much more than that. A confidant, advisor, friend, inspirator; his need for this noble bird went beyond normal friendship, there was a spiritual connection now that linked him to a world, he knew little

159

about but hinted at purpose. Yes, this bird was so much more than his protector.

He started the walk back not looking forward to life in the cave for the immediate future. Somehow it was different, he was different; unsure how to continue after what had happened, unable to communicate because they had asked for time. And the security, he'd felt at being part of the family, seemed severed. For the first time in a long time Yiska didn't know what to do, what to say and how he could even look them in the eyes. He was ashamed, and everything he'd been through, adapted to and learnt seemed irrelevant. He felt lost.

Chapter 24:
Whirlpool Mind

Nayati headed deep into the woods, walking at a pace that matched his mood. He stumbled several times when the snow beneath his feet gave way to hidden depths. Because of this he slowed, seeking to find a place of shelter. It wasn't long before he came to the spot that Yiska and Doli had dug into the incline.

Fresh snow had almost closed the entrance, and he almost didn't see it but, as he stopped to examine it, he couldn't help but admire the industry that created it in such appalling conditions.

He opened the entrance and crawled through. Built for two, there was plenty of room for him and his meagre belongings. He placed them inside before going out again.

The small hand axe, attached to his belt, rubbed against his leg and he head off into the forest to cut wood. Several trips later, there was sufficient for a few days. Then, just as it was getting dark, he struck his fire stick and a blaze of bright-orange sparks rained down on the tinder he had readied. It caught, and he carefully added pieces of wood, increasing in size, as each took the flame, until the fire was as good as that in the cave at home.

He took his food pack and pulled out one of the smoked trout from within and impaled it on a long thin stick. He drove the other end deep into the snow at an angle leaning towards the fire for it to warm through and then set a small container packed with snow to melt alongside.

It wasn't long before he was eating fish and drinking herbal tea. In reality, the anger he'd been experiencing had dissipated a long while ago, but he hadn't noticed it while he had been setting up camp. Now that he'd finished the work his mind was free again, and it wandered onto recent events.

Why was it that his grandfather and sister could not see the risk in bringing Yiska to their home? Could they not see the disrespect that he showed for their culture? Did they not understand that you couldn't train a westerner to become a Navajo?

His mind engaged a multitude of smaller, less significant questions that simmered, but always it came back to those first three. He dealt with them one at a time.

Yiska would leave sometime soon, it was inevitable, if his memories hadn't returned. He would seek the knowledge of his past and leave to search for it. It was the natural thing to do. They had shown him where they lived, how they live in a place where others had rules to say that they couldn't. If Yiska said the wrong thing to the wrong person then life, as his family knew it, would end.

No man, brought up as a Westerner, could ever show true respect to the Navajo culture. It is alien from their customs. Complicated, different and full of small ways of behaviour, understood only through years of living it. Yiska is at one with the Western ways, we all know this. It is the way, not even his fault, that he keeps doing the wrong things, shows no respect. He cannot

162

learn because he needed to learn these ways as a child. He tries, but this is just to please Doli and Niyol. How he is with Doli shows this. He wants to live like a Navajo and yet does western things, despite being told this is not their way. There is no point, and we should send him away. But that wouldn't work because he could betray their whereabouts.

The turmoil continued and Nayati spent most of the night in front of the fire before tiredness broke the cycle of torment in his mind and he retired to the shelter for sleep. He slept only for brief periods though.

The next day brought little peace to his troubled mind and followed a similar route as the first with no answers disclosing themselves. Again, torturous thoughts murdered his sleep and kept him from resting.

On the third day however, Nayati broke the trend by imagining he was alone with Niyol and asking him the questions that he couldn't find the answers too. *What would the old man say?*

Acting out a roleplay in his mind with an imaginary Niyol he opened the questions into a broader format that allowed him to question the questions. For the first time Nayati questioned his own thinking. It could be flawed by the emotions he felt.

Niyol would tell him to look deeper, talk to the spirits even, but Nayati had little experience of getting answers from the spirits. The spirits raised even more questions.

By the time he retired to the snow shelter on the third night the process of deep thought had exhausted him, along with the lack of sleep and the daily routine of survival work. He had answers of a kind though.

It was snowing when he woke, late the next morning. Outside his shelter, it was almost a whiteout, but the flakes were falling vertical which meant little wind. The fire had gone out, and he relit it, his task made easier because the embers still held heat. Taking out the last of his food, he ate.

There was no choice but to return home tonight, late though, to avoid too much conversation. He knew there was more to think about, but it was getting easier and he consoled himself that if he'd been acting unreasonably; it had been for the right reasons. Unlike Doli, Nayati followed the ways of his grandfather, he didn't talk openly before he had examined every aspect. Yiska had let his actions speak for him when he first came to their home, so perhaps he could do the same. Perhaps it would be better this way.

There was something else on his mind now though. He had to face Yiska and had no idea that Yiska felt as lost as he did. How he could look him in the eye was uncertain. In recent months it was the second time that Nayati had been in a situation that threatened his confidence in his own ability. At the market those who did not like him being of mixed spirits had threatened him; he had worried about how he would have reacted if Uncle Fred had not been around. And now it was Yiska who had threatened his position, only he'd taken it a step further, showing that he wasn't capable of holding his own in a physical situation.

As he prepared to leave the cave, he knew that life was going to be difficult for a while and for the first time realised that it wasn't just others who might have to adapt or change. He might have to.

Chapter 25:
It's Mine, Not Yours!

Nayati returned home late evening, just before it was time to sleep. Niyol and Doli greeted him and enquired about his general well-being. Yiska averted his eyes but said it pleased him to see him return. Doli passed him a tea, and the greetings were minimal. Nayati had planned for this, and Niyol and Doli understood this was what he would need.

Sensitivity subdued the next few days at the cave allowing time to heal the recent rifts. More prolonged snowfall had kept them inside and the tension in the air was clear. Yiska and Nayati had made brief eye contact but had not spoken.

Niyol and Doli had done their best to include both boys in everything and had spread their attention equally. Niyol wondered how long it would be before the trouble between the boys reared up again and he made sure that he kept both busy.

Yiska watched carefully while Niyol made new arrows. Niyol selected a long, almost straight stick from the bundle that lay in front of him. He heated it carefully above any natural bend, before flexing it against the curvature between his fingers and thumbs. Looking down its length he assessed the straightness before reheating and straightening further.

Whilst he did this, Nayati opened a pouch full of arrowheads, carved from the leg bones of deer that had once provided meat for the family. Taking the shaft that Niyol had straightened, he cut the length to match an arrow he used as a guide. Then cutting a slit at one end with his knife, he inserted an arrowhead. He bound a length of thin sinew around the shaft to hold the arrowhead in place. Next, he dipped a thin stick into a pot heating by the fire, containing tree resin and ground down charcoal. He spread the mixture carefully, thick and even onto the sinew, before laying the arrow down to dry.

Yiska took a stick from Niyol's collection and examined the imperfections in it. He looked to Niyol and gestured towards the fire. Niyol nodded encouragement and sat back to watch Yiska's efforts. He hadn't selected the best stick within the bundle; there were several imperfections to straighten. Ironing out one imperfection he passed it to Niyol to inspect.

Niyol accepted it and stared down the length. He nodded and returned it to Yiska. Again, Yiska looked down the shaft then held it out over the fire to apply heat. After a few seconds he withdrew it and straightened out another imperfection. He repeated the process twice more before running his eyes down the length and offering it back to Niyol. Once more Niyol glanced down the length and then laid it on the ground. He rolled the arrow shaft along the ground and watched it rotate smooth and even. He picked it up and looked at Yiska.

"It would seem you have the skill for this task," he said in approval.

Nayati, who had been watching Yiska with interest, selected one of his arrowheads and passed it to him. Yiska took his knife, sliced a slit in the end of his arrow shaft and inserted the head. Nayati passed him a length of sinew and watched as Yiska bound it.

This time Yiska passed the shaft to Nayati who inspected it and returned it with a small nod. Reaching for the stick he had used from the pot, he passed it to Yiska who applied the glue and when he finished the task, he laid his arrow down.

Niyol observed the interchange and smiled to himself. It's a start!

Doli called Yiska over to her and instructed him to watch the next stage of the process. She selected an arrow her brother had made and then a feather from a long thin drawstring pouch. She showed how to apply the feather to the end of the shaft, twisting it round. Then she took some of the thinnest sinew that Yiska had ever seen and whipped this round the stem of the feather attaching it firmly to the shaft. She knotted the end and trimmed it off.

Then, with a finer stick than her brother had used, she applied some sticky mixture carefully over the sinew. She told Yiska that he must get none of the mixture on the feather itself as this would affect the way the arrow flew. Then she selected a rather beautiful eagle feather from her collection and offered it to Yiska. He followed her example and completed the task to her approval.

"In the spring, you will make your own bow," said Niyol, pleased with his work. "If there is no snow tonight, we will hunt tomorrow," the old man told them. "We will go to the far side of the mountain where deer may be present. The travel will be hard and slow for we cannot use the litter with Friend. We will stay for two nights if the deer are difficult to find, the need to find more food for winter before it snows again is great."

They all nodded in agreement and continued making arrows.

That evening Doli cooked additional food for the hunting trip. It was easier to take food for reheating at speed in such cold and difficult conditions.

Friend would carry most of their supplies in packs on his back, enabling them to move unencumbered on the snow. Success on the hunt would mean they would carry these packs themselves on the way back, whilst Friend would carry their deer. They all looked forward to the trip and retired early that night.

At first light the following morning they ate a hearty meal before setting out. Each had their own duties: Doli took care of food, Nayati the weapons, Niyol blankets and sleeping mats, and Yiska fetched Friend.

The cold air outside was bitter and the normal matt-white blanket of fresh snow had changed. It sparkled like millions of sequins, and a crust had formed that crunched underfoot before giving way to the softer snow beneath. The temperature had plummeted overnight transforming the landscape again. Just like the snow on the ground sparkled, so did the trees, bushes and shrubs. A magical fairyland in the Arizona mountain forest.

Within an hour they'd sealed the cave, and the journey was underway. Yiska was not looking forward to being outside at night in temperatures this cold but the others had done this many times before. Nayati led the way on foot with Yiska behind and Niyol, Doli and Friend bringing up the rear. With less than two-hundred yards covered Yiska suddenly slumped lifeless to the ground. It took a full two seconds before Niyol and Doli realised that he hadn't just tripped, and something was wrong. Niyol called to Nayati, who hadn't seen Yiska fall, to stop.

This time, the boy was older. Again, he was sitting in the large room, with the contents of his box on the bed beside him. Examining the letter, he watched the words dance before him on the page.

He wished that he could read or had somebody to read the letter to him. The words had to be important but there wasn't anybody he could trust.

Placing the letter and the other items back in the box, he closed the lid, placing it back into the drawer and locked it. The only possessions, apart from a few clothes, he could say were his. Since he'd arrived at this place, he had nothing else.

As he lay back, a voice at the other end of the room spoke.

"I want that box and all the things inside it."

The voice was familiar and as he turned, he saw a tall, stocky, silhouette approaching him, blocking off the sunlight that poured in through the window. He felt himself shake with dread and fear.

"You can't have it; it's mine, not yours!" he replied, in a voice he hoped did not sound afraid, as the shape loomed ever closer towards him.

Yiska opened his eyes and saw three concerned faces peering down at him. He felt the pain inside his head and moaned.

"You saw more visions, Yiska?" Niyol asked.

Yiska nodded and moaned as the pain inside his head became worse.

Nayati pulled away, signalling Niyol to follow.

"We cannot take him on the hunt," Nayati started. "If he falls again, it will be difficult to care for him away from the cave. Yet we must hunt before the snows return."

169

"This is true. We will hunt alone Grandson. Yiska will return to the cave and Doli will stay with him; there is no better person to care for him and he will be safe," Niyol returned.

They moved back to Yiska and Doli.

"Can you walk, Yiska? You cannot stay longer on the snow, for your body will cool and you will become sick," said Niyol.

Yiska said he would try, so Nayati and Niyol helped him up. He felt dizzy and was unsteady on his feet. The two of them helped him back to the cave, supporting his weight between them. Doli unsealed it and relit the fire and when Yiska settled Nayati and Niyol departed and descended the mountain.

"I am sorry you can't go on the hunt, Doli, I know you were looking forward to it," Yiska told her.

"Do not concern yourself with this, there will be many more," she replied.

Yiska closed his eyes and slept until the following morning when, once again, he woke to Doli's smiling face.

"You slept long Yiska, how do you feel?"

"My head is better now but I feel weak," he replied.

"You need to eat and drink, for you have taken nothing since yesterday," she told him.

He ate the food and drink she offered him without sitting up.

She always knows what to do, thought Yiska, realising how hungry he was. She watched him eat and smiled as he told her he felt better and sat up.

"Thank you for looking after me again, Doli," he said.

She nodded without replying, pleased at his comment.

"You would talk about what you saw?" she asked.

170

"Not yet."

Doli had been weaving another basket while he slept and continued her work on it as he watched. After a while he rose and went outside. It was still bitter, although it had not snowed further, but the wind had picked up and stung his face. He shivered and went back inside.

"Is there anything we need, more wood or something?" he asked her.

"We have all we need," she replied. "In the autumn, we prepare well for these cold times. It is a time to rest, like the animals that sleep through it."

"I feel restless, I need to be doing something," Yiska said.

"You could clean the shelter for Friend and lay more straw ready for her return. The journey will tire her, and she will need to rest," Doli suggested.

Yiska nodded, put on his over-blanket and went outside. He enjoyed the quiet as he walked to the enclosure.

Finishing the tasks Doli had suggested, he added fresh hay to the bundle already tied there for food before making his way back to the cave. He glanced up to see the eagle soaring high above and said a word of thanks for its protection.

His head cleared, and he wondered how many more visions he would have. The impact this was having on the rest of the family, with plans altered at short notice worried him. All of them made contributions towards the burden of survival, and he did not wish to burden them by being unable to do what they needed.

"When will the others will return?" he asked Doli.

"When they finish what they do," she replied with confidence. "It is the way here. A task takes as long as it needs."

He nodded, "I wish I was contributing too."

"We all help in different ways, Yiska. There are times when we help and times when we do not. Do not trouble yourself with such thoughts."

"It has been a while since we have shared time alone."

"It is true what you say and there has been reason for this."

"You mean the fight between me and Nayati?"

"Yes, but also other things."

"What things?"

"The weather, being in the cave for long periods, winter tasks and healing time."

"When my brother returned home, it is the way of things that Niyol and I spend time with you and he in amounts that balance. In this way you will know, and he will know that we keep no bad feeling for you. No man can change the past. If you learn from this, then good can come from it."

"You're as wise as your grandfather; I miss the closeness that we shared Doli, it has been so long since we held hands or kissed."

"This we cannot do when we are with others."

Yiska's heart slumped, and he stopped talking. Doli seemed to guess how he was feeling and continued.

"We cannot do this when we are with others," she repeated. "I miss this too."

Yiska's face erupted into an enormous smile and he moved closer to her. For a moment she averted her eyes from contacting his, before succumbing to the draw. Yiska lifted her chin upwards and gazed deep into them and she felt the sheer penetrating force. He leant forward and pressed his lips to hers and wrapped his arms around her.

Chapter 26:
Spirit Animal

Down the mountainside, Nayati and Niyol were tracking a large female deer. They'd been fortunate, for the further they had travelled down, the less snow they'd encountered and there was just a few inches beneath their feet. The hunt so far had been successful, and they already had one deer that lay over Friend's back, as they started their return journey.

On route, they had stumbled over a second animal's tracks, and as they were fresh, they'd taken a chance and followed them. If they were fortunate in shooting a second deer, life would be much easier during the coming months.

Nayati tracked the animal, whilst Niyol led Friend some distance behind, and after an hour he saw his prey at last. There, at the edge of a small glade, the deer was clearing snow with her nose, to feed on grass beneath.

He took his time in approach, careful not to make a single sound. Although the snow here was soft, and muffled sound, he still put his foot down slowly on its outer edge, gradually rolling it over flat to reduce any noise further. Testing the wind direction, he found relief that it was still coming from the side, as it had been when he first tracked the animal.

He removed the bow he had been carrying across his shoulder and selected an arrow. Cover from the surrounding shrubs and trees allowed him to close to within thirty yards, another ten-yard gain would ensure that his arrow would fly deep into the flesh.

The foliage was dense here, and he crouched behind a thin bush. The animal looked up, ears twitching, straining, as if some sixth sense had warned it that something was wrong; it listened for sounds. Nayati held his breath and waited for the animal to graze again, before slowly raising his bow and taking aim. The animal rose from its feeding and Nayati once more waited, for what seemed like an eternity. As the deer lowered his head once more, Nayati released his arrow. It flew fast striking the deer, but the deer took flight with the arrow still attached.

Nayati cursed, for he'd struck the animal less than two inches from its heart; for him it was a bad shot. He gave chase, an injured animal might run for several miles before it succumbed to its wound.

Niyol followed behind, tracking Nayati's trail; his footprints visible in the snow and it was not long before he found the place where Nayati had taken his shot. He then noticed the increased gait of Nayati's footprints, and read that his grandson was giving chase, which meant he hadn't achieved a clean kill. He also knew that the deer might run for some distance and noticed with a frown at the direction that would take them further away from home than they had already travelled.

Nayati would not leave a wounded animal in the woods to suffer a slow death any more than Niyol would; His people took only took what they needed from the forest and nothing more. They respected and honoured the creatures they shared their home with.

After an hour of travelling, Niyol caught up with Nayati who greeted him with a smile. He saw the deer on the ground in front of Nayati and nodded his approval. His grandson had already given thanks to the spirits for his prize and removed the internal organs from the deer. It was not long before they secured the second deer on top of the first, on Friend's back, and the journey home began.

Niyol estimated they were a day and a half away, another night to camp out. It had been bitter cold the previous night, and both had slept in the travelling tepee, close to the fire. Another night like that was not welcome but there was little choice, and they travelled well into the darkness. The moon was full and some of its light reached through the trees to reflect on the snow. In a clearing, with frost sparkling in the moonlight, they stopped to make camp, eat and rest.

Niyol awoke first after achieving little sleep and his old bones ached from the cold. It was getting increasingly difficult to do things he'd done all his life; it was fortunate that Nayati was old enough to take on the physical tasks.

Warm food, heated by the fire, was the last that Doli had prepared for them and after, when they settled for the night, he watched his grandson sleep. Proud of his capable nature and that he'd grown up respecting the traditional ways of his people, he valued the stability of his family. In some ways it was not surprising he saw Yiska as a threat to that stability. *He is almost a man, he thought.*

Thoughts turned to Yiska, and he wondered how the relationship between him and Nayati would develop. He still hoped they would become friends; they would balance each other. How much longer would it be before Nayati accepted that he liked Yiska and found peace with that knowledge.

The other night, Yiska made the arrow for the first time. Nayati had not ridiculed his efforts, the arrow was of good quality, in truth there was nothing to ridicule. Was this a sign of change? He hoped so; he would speak to Nayati about this. Perhaps it was time to bring up the subject while they were still alone.

Half an hour later they were on the move again, taking a diagonal course away from the direction they had followed the deer on, to intersect their original trail. As they headed up the mountain, the snow thickened, slowing the pace of their journey.

Nayati held up his hand, a signal to stop.

"What is it Nayati?" Niyol asked.

"It is my thinking we are not alone," he said, scanning the forest in all directions.

Niyol said nothing, but experience had taught him to listen to such feelings. They continued for a while until Nayati stopped again. This time he was more emphatic.

"We are not alone, of this I am sure," he warned.

As he finished speaking, there came the unmistakable cry of an eagle. Nayati looked up and saw it flying, high above, as it called again.

"It is Yiska's eagle; there must be trouble at home. Something is wrong!" said Nayati, his worried face matching the concern in his voice.

"There is no problem at home for the bird would not leave him, they have safety in the cave," said Niyol, as the bird cried out again.

"The problem is here, Old Man. Look there!" Nayati called, pointing to a bush at the edge of the clearing, his hand already reaching for his knife.

176

The leaves were rustling, ominous in the lack of wind. Niyol withdrew his knife too, and the two of them watched with apprehension.

With a blood-curdling snarl the bush burst open, and a mountain cat burst out and ambled towards them, its huge paws silent as it placed them carefully on the ground.

Nayati felt a prickling as the hairs on the back of his neck stood up.

"That is the lion we met before, see the black mark under its eye," he hissed.

"You are right, but now it looks hungry. See how thin it is!" Niyol responded, a thin sheen of sweat forming above his upper lip despite the cold.

The beast's ribs and hips prominent as its skin sagged from its frame. It took another step forward, and they noticed it limp on one of its back legs. Niyol pulled on Friend's reins as she backed away in agitation.

Nayati edged backwards towards the mare as the mountain cat took another step forward with an angry growl. Its eyes glazed and focussed on the two deer, hanging across the horses' back.

"Do not move, Nayati!" ordered Niyol, but Nayati continued to edge backwards.

As he reached Friend he turned and, with the expertise of a butcher, cut off the hind leg from one deer, snapping the joint that held it to the carcass. He flung the heavy limb as far as he possible towards the snarling cat. It fell short, and the cat continued to walk towards them.

"Take it and go, great cat, for there is meat here to feed us all," Nayati yelled at it.

The cat picked up the deer haunch in its mouth, turned and stalked away, revealing a large seeping wound on the back of one leg.

"You did not use our ways Nayati?" Niyol stated, as they stood there. "An injured cat, as well as hungry, it was dangerous."

"Yiska!" was all that Nayati said, before looking up and thanking the eagle high above.

They travelled once more but a short while later, Niyol asked.

"What do you mean, Yiska?"

"It is my thoughts that the eagle is Yiska's spirit bird and he sent it to me as a warning. I have seen Yiska do many strange things, and he has a way that makes bad, become good!"

"At the cave, he wanted no harm to the great cat, the cat left. I used his ways. The cat was thin and hungry, I gave it food; it left us unharmed. This is Yiska's way."

Niyol paused before responding. "You learn quick as Yiska, and your thoughts are right, except..."

He paused a little, a tease, before Nayati said. "Speak your thoughts, Old Man!"

Again, Niyol paused, building suspense. "It is not, so that Yiska sent his eagle to help you. You have the same spirit animal as he! The eagle is also Doli's spirit animal."

Nayati stopped and stared at Niyol. "The eagle is a powerful spirit, Old Man. You say it is rare for such a powerful guide and now we all share the same?"

"Yiska has many gifts," said Niyol "But he does not have power to send his spirit animal to you and he would not know you were in trouble. At the cave, the bird guards each of you. This is what I think; the eagle is your spirit guide too! You are on a journey that is as one with your sister and Yiska. I am not knowing for how long, but I am certain it is as I say," he finished.

Nayati gave it consideration as they continued up the mountain. He hoped that Niyol was right, and he often was. He understood how fortunate he would be to have such a powerful spirit guide and hoped this was the case. When they reached a clearing, Nayati looked up to see if the eagle was present, but it had gone, at least for now.

They made good time despite the increasing depth of snow, and Niyol estimated that they should reach the cave just after dark.

Nayati was looking forward to telling the story of feeding the great cat, and his newfound spirit animal while Niyol was musing about the comforts of home, of eating some of Doli's cooking and having a good night's rest. He also wanted to check on Yiska's health, to learn about his latest visions, and work out their significance. Always there is too much work, he thought before remembering his earlier thoughts and deciding to broach the subject now.

Chapter 27:
Issues of Trust

"There is something I would talk with you about. It is a matter of concern and affects all those who live at the cave."

"Speak of this Old Man." Nayati replied.

"The Dineh live in peace; family is most important, and we honour respect between men, would you not agree?"

"It should be as you say for this is what you have taught me Grandfather."

"Why is there no respect from you to Yiska? It has been a worry for some time. He has done nothing to deserve the way you treat him."

Nayati's head lowered, he did not want to talk about this. A scowl erupted on his face. He pondered carefully before answering.

"Perhaps Grandfather it is for me and Yiska to find our way," his answer trying to thwart further discussion.

"I would agree that this should be the way but, there is doubt in my mind this will happen. Understand what is between you concerns others. This saddens Doli and is the same with me. The journey you share would have trails that are easier to follow if you were at one with the other."

"It is difficult for me to be as you want. I am becoming a man and have ideas of my own thinking. Much of what I know comes from the teachings of my Grandfather and yet my own thoughts are from you."

"What is your meaning?"

"You have taught me that men of the western world are not like Navajo. There are some who would take me away from the old man I care about. The people are not as one with the world or each other. Is this not their way?"

"It is the way of some. Even with the Navajo there are some who break traditions."

"If this is true, I trust none from the world outside our home?"

"We should judge each man on his actions and the things he says."

"This I know Grandfather. Yiska has no memories. He has no actions to trust."

"This is no fault of his, you are witness to the injuries he had, how close to entering the spirit world he came. Think how he is with us. He has tried to honour our ways. You acted with the great cat using his way."

"He does not honour my sister as he should."

"He has feelings for Doli, not those for a sister. Doli has feelings for him. He is of western ways first and he tries to be as us from choice."

"I cannot respect the western ways he has. The way he is with Doli is not respectful."

"This is because you are not western. You have little understanding of Yiska's ways. You are different and have no need here. If you leave our home to follow your life journey, you will need such knowledge."

"I have no plans to leave our home."

"It is the way of life to journey; how will you find a woman to share your journey with?"

"I need no woman."

"In time you will Nayati."

Nayati fell silent hoping this conversation had ended, but it hadn't.

"You do not trust Yiska, I understand your thinking. But what is there not to like?"

Nayati didn't answer and Niyol pushed harder.

"Your way with Yiska is not good. Why is this so Nayati?"

"He tries to be one of us, but he is not; our family is not his; what does he do for us to earn what we have given him?"

"He is of mixed spirits as you are, as Doli is. You are a family of a different kind. All he does is for the good of family. He learns the skills of our people well. The skills he learns, he is as you in some, not as you in others and is better in some, yet he has only a short while to learn these things."

"He is not as I am, and he will not be as I am!"

Niyol suddenly recognised the truth behind Nayati's actions. It wasn't just about respecting and honouring the culture. Nayati worried that Yiska would outperform him and devalue his worth. Yiska threatened his status.

"It is the way of life that each man has some skills but not others. No man has all and no man has none. It is so that Yiska is better in some things than Nayati and some things that he is not. You must honour this. By doing so, you might call upon him to help you and he might call upon you in the same way."

"Yiska is not better at anything."

"You are not with truth about yourself. The race in the forest, he runs like the wind. You know he should

182

have beaten you. Instead, he spares you defeat. His arrow was at one with yours and yet it was his first. There is a calmness about him, he is patient. You are headstrong and sometimes act without thought, this shows what you say is wrong. Life is about using different skills that help on the journey. Not all skills are from one man. You are not the same, you are different, each has value. Think hard on this grandson and change your way with him. Think how strong you are with him at your side. It is easier to be a friend with one you respect even if you wish that it isn't so. When you hear the truth in what I say you will choose the right path. This I know. I have said enough on this matter."

Nayati felt betrayed by what his grandfather had said. He hadn't understood what he had tried to say. He felt like he sometimes did when he was younger, and his stubborn ways had incurred a rebuke from Niyol. The lessons were painful then, and they were painful now.

I am no longer a child and my thoughts should be of worth and yet they do not hear he thought, and the anger simmered inside threatening to erupt. He fought to keep it down.

When they reached home Nayati butchered the animals alone to avoid any contact with the others. The work gave him focus, quelling his troubled mind. His earlier thoughts of sharing the story about the mountain lion had long since vanished and he finished late in the evening just in time for bed.

Chapter 28:
Feelings

It was soon after dawn when Doli passed Niyol his early morning drink. Nayati and Yiska slept on. Away from the fire the cold from outside tried to permeate their home, they moved closer to it.

"Old Man, I would talk to you about things inside of me. This we must do alone." Doli informed Niyol.

"When Yiska and your brother awake it will be as you say."

The manner of her delivery made it quite clear to Niyol she didn't want to wait for too long. The boys woke a few minutes later.

"It would please me if you walk with me for a while Grandfather."

"It would please me also Bluebird since it has been a while since we shared time alone."

Niyol had already guessed what the proposed discussion involved and used her translated name to show she had his entire attention.

An hour later they left the cave after donning their outer blankets. Neither said anything to Yiska or Nayati who were both busy fetching more wood for the inner cave store. They simply waved an announcement they were off somewhere for a while.

Doli did not try to start the conversation wanting to wait until away from the boys. Niyol guessed the reason for her prolonged silence and waited with infinite patience. They rounded a bend on an incline and Doli stopped at a boulder, located under the canopy of an old pine.

It had rolled there millenniums ago, and the tree just grew alongside it. A suitable place to stop, as the boulder had a flattened top with only a small layer of snow upon it. She brushed it off and sat down, indicating for Niyol to sit alongside her.

Still, he refrained from speaking, knowing instinctively she searched for a way to broach what bothered her. Doli had no idea that her grandfather knew already.

"Grandfather it is my thinking I have dishonoured the Navajo traditions with what I feel and what I have done. I am lost in this."

Niyol spotted a tear form and then fall from her eyes which remained focussed toward her feet.

"Tell me Granddaughter, what is it you have done that causes you to feel this way."

"Nayati is right in saying that I bring dishonour to the ways of our people. I have allowed Yiska to be close to me. We have held hands; we have kissed and although he taught me these things, I would like that he does it more. Our traditions forbid this and yet I seek more."

"It is not wrong Doli to seek a mate. The spirits expect this, and all creatures seek this. Some mate for a small time, some for longer."

"I did not know that I was seeking a mate. I know just that I feel different inside about Yiska than I do Nayati."

"It is normal to seek a mate without knowing this. Age is not of importance. You have no learning of seeing others experience what you are thinking and feeling, for you it is harder to recognise this for what it is."

"How is it you know what I feel, I have not shared this with you?"

"Signs, those who felt this before recognise this in others. The feelings between people are common."

"You have had these feelings?"

Niyol smiled. "A story of one man and one woman comes to mind and this will help you understand."

"What is happening to me and why is it I wish to break the ways of our people."

"Before I start, you will hear me when I say that you do not dishonour the ways of the people but honour the gifts the spirits give each of us. Do you hear me Doli?"

"I hear you."

Niyol smiled and searched for a place to start his story. There was so much he could share but the details were not as important as the feelings at this moment.

"In times long past, a young man walked by a stream lost in thoughts of travel. Travel away from the reservation to places unseen before. There are those who stay on the reservation for life, content with this, but this man wanted more. He had become without patience, needing to leave and was planning the day he would turn away from what he knew."

"Movement ahead captured his attention, and his thoughts lost focus as he moved towards it. As he arrived, the movement formed into a woman who stood as he drew close. She looked up and smiled and the face showed she smiled all the time. The beauty, in her face, caused him to stop breathing. Her smile made him stare for longer than our customs permit. Her smile made his stomach feel tight as it does when you are sick or with

186

fear. Her smile made him want to stay with her and he did not understand why. And her smile stole the words from his mouth, and when she greeted him, he could not find an answer."

"What he felt warned he was not thinking or feeling in the traditional ways, but he was thinking and feeling in the way of those blessed with love from the spirits, although he did not know of this."

"What happened?"

"He tried to greet the woman, but his words were unclear, and he was uncomfortable with this. But she did not laugh at this. She spoke with the music of the Bluebird."

"The man forgot his thoughts of travel and spent the rest of the day with her. He was a child with her, difficulty with speaking stayed true for the afternoon, as he found more to like about her."

"She moved with the grace of an eagle and with the lightness of foot of a mountain lion on the hunt. She had a smell like a mountain meadow flower, the violet ones that flower for many weeks. Her hair danced about her face catching the sunlight which shone red through the black. It bounced up and down at the shoulders in the breeze like a new-born deer testing out its running legs."

"For many cycles of the sun the man no longer thought of travel. He found different reasons to seek the woman out and remain at her side. Soon there was no need of this, and everybody accepted the pairing."

"This is how I feel when I am with Yiska. He likes the way my hair bounces too."

"I have seen this when you are together, and I believe it is how he feels about you."

"How is it that I honour the spirits and dishonour the Dineh at the same time?"

187

"The dishonour you feel is in your mind only. It is not my thoughts that you dishonour anything. It is my thinking that Yiska feels this way too."

"Nayati is different, as a brother he tries only to protect you and is proud to live in the manner he does."

"The way he thinks has come from my teachings, but he has understood my words as unbreakable rules. He does not seek to learn the things between what is and what is not. His bond to you is strong for you are twins and I sense jealousy, that you wish to spend your time with Yiska more so than him."

"But it is not as I wish; I want to spend time with him, but he uses tasks so that it does not happen."

"It is his way of dealing with the bad feelings he has inside."

"I want him to see what I see in Yiska, for them to be friends."

"Nayati wants to be friends, he is not understanding this yet. It is my thinking that in time they will become as brothers."

Doli fell silent for a while as she contemplated what Niyol had shared with her. After a while she broke the silence.

"The man and woman in the story, you and Grandmother?"

"It is as you say."

"Is it true that she made you feel like the words you say, or did you say this to make me feel better?"

"Your grandmother made me feel in ways that no other has. I have trouble with breathing every time I was with her. Her beauty takes my heart and squeezes it."

"I thought that I was the most beautiful one in your life." Doli smiled.

"You, your mother and your grandmother all squeeze my heart. You are alike in good ways."

"It pleases me that you have shared this with me Old Man."

"When there is trouble in your mind, it pleases me that you come to me still. Be with Yiska in ways that are right with you, but spare this from your brother when he present. He is not understanding of these matters."

"We should go back."

"We should, but it would please me to take a longer journey back," he smiled.

Chapter 29:
Peace, of a Sort

It was noon by the time they returned and found Yiska practising with the bow. Nayati was nowhere apparent.

"You are improving Yiska, each day of practise brings you nearer to matching the skill Nayati and I have."

"I will keep trying." Yiska answered but his eyes had fallen on Doli, and his own smile mirrored the one that radiated from her face.

"There is no lasting problem from your latest visit to the spirits. If it agrees with you, I would listen to what you learned."

"I'll collect my arrows and then tell you what I learned." Yiska answered.

"We need a warm drink so let us go inside."

"There is pine needle tea close to the fire, it just needs warming," Doli stated.

"You are a gift from the spirits granddaughter."

Just as they turned toward the cave, Nayati appeared carrying an axe in his hand.

"You accepted the challenge of responsibility this winter and it pleases me to watch you share the demands of living in this way." Niyol told him, witnessing the pleasure of his words hit home as Nayati stiffened and nodded.

"We are to learn of Yiska's latest visit to the spirit world. It would please me if you share your thoughts on this." Nayati halted.

"Why is it you seek my thoughts on this matter, I have little knowledge of the spirit world to draw from?"

"You fast become a man Nayati, with ways of thinking different from my own. You think as the young; it is the way and your thoughts are of equal importance. Will you do this for me?"

"It will be as you say Grandfather."

"Tell me about the hunt first." Yiska requested. "Those two deer you prepared last night were something else."

Once settled Nayati described the details of the hunt which he did with clarity.

Yiska could visualise everything he described, "I had no idea you could tell such great stories, Nayati, and I admire your hunting skills. I look forward to the day when you can share your knowledge with me on a hunt," Yiska told him.

Nayati could not hide his pleasure at the praise Yiska gave him and promised to teach him the skills his grandfather had taught him. He teased by saying it might take time!

Niyol looked at him, surprised. *That's the second time!*

Niyol took over the storytelling now and described the return visit by the great cat. Sparing no details, he mirrored his grandson with the skill of his delivery; telling of the eagle and the way Nayati had offered the mountain lion food and related the reasons Nayati had given for his action. The actions of his grandson and the bravery he had displayed were commendable. Then he asked Yiska for his thoughts on the matter.

Once again Yiska complimented Nayati and then offered his own views, adopting a little of the manner in which the other members of the family spoke.

"It pleases me to share the same spirit animal with you, for you have many qualities that show you deserve a high-status spirit to guide you. I am also pleased that, at such a difficult moment, you chose the path I would, if I had been in the same situation. The respect you showed for the mountain lion will please the spirits, Nayati, and I am proud of your actions."

Nayati responded, "My Grandfather taught me you learn from all, it pleases me to have such a wise Grandfather, for the knowledge I gain from him serves me well."

It was the third time Nayati had made a positive comment towards Yiska and again it didn't go unnoticed. Yiska nodded in agreement.

Niyol asked Doli how long Yiska had taken to awaken from his last vision and how he had been when he awoke. He appeared unconcerned with her answers, stating there was little they could do about it, and that there were no long-lasting side effects to these events. He focussed on Yiska and nodded a request to start. When Yiska had recounted what he had seen, he asked Niyol what conclusions he had drawn.

Niyol started with his customary pause. "There is no doubt in my mind these are your memories being returned," he started, stating the obvious.

Nayati interrupted. "Forgive my interruption, Grandfather, but it is my thoughts the memories move forwards in time; this person in Yiska's dream could be the one who did him harm."

"These are my thoughts also, Nayati, but Yiska's injuries came from more than one. This was clear from the injuries themselves. It is only time and his spirit guide that separates Yiska from his memories. Their return may be hard to bear as not all the memories will be good."

Yiska nodded in agreement. "I agree," he said. "I still don't know who I was."

Doli spoke up. "Until you get this knowledge, you are Yiska of the Navajo. You are one with us as family. You respect life as we do. It does not matter who you were, it matters only who you are now. You are Yiska of the Navajo!"

"It is so that my sister speaks beyond her years on this earth, she is wise and thoughtful, and it pleases me that she can share this with us," Nayati stated, paying his sister a rare compliment.

Niyol felt surprise and significance at the moment. Nayati was making an apology to his sister in his own unique manner but, more than that, was giving her his acceptance about how she felt about Yiska. There was also a concession there towards Yiska, perhaps the first real sign that his views might be changing. Niyol turned his attention toward Doli, pleased at what she said.

"It is true what Doli says," he said confirming Nayati's statement. "Even the knowledge of the person you were, cannot change the person you are becoming, for this is more important. What ever happened in the past, good or bad, shapes the way you become now."

Yiska looked at them both and nodded.

"I respect what you're saying, it's wise and true, but I still need to find out though," he said, frustration clear.

Later during the evening Yiska was looking out over the drop-off illuminated by the full moon. It was a spectacular view; some of the canopy had shed its burden of snow, creating a moonscape-like quality, stretching as far as the eye could perceive. The wind, had been stiffening all day, adding to the fall in temperature and bringing a chill factor of well below freezing. Doli came to fetch him but Yiska wanted a few more moments.

"What holds your eyes Yiska?" she asked.

He placed his arm around her he answered. "This place, the beauty, the isolation, the loneliness and more, I don't have the words for everything I feel."

"It is as home?"

"It is, but I'm always wondering what I've left behind. Good or bad, somewhere else was home once."

"The loneliness, is this you inside?"

"Yes. Not a loneliness as in being alone, but for who I am and where I come from. I'm lonely for myself. There is so much missing."

Doli said nothing but pulled at his over-blanket forcing him to lower his head and meet her lips. The warmth flooded his body, and he crushed her against him.

The wind persisted for two weeks, and the snow returned with fury. It confined them to the cave for most of that period, content in finding time to make several things with which to trade, during the spring.

Yiska made an excellent pupil and surprised them all with the way he learned so quickly. Niyol shared many stories with him, each revealing the ways of the Navajo. Yiska listened to them with genuine pleasure, working out the concealed messages for himself before sharing his thoughts with Niyol.

Nayati and Yiska had taken turns each day to clear snow from the cave entrance. There was now several feet against the front wall of the cave, blown by the wind into a steep slope which tapered off at the cliff edge.

They kept the narrow chimney clear with stout sticks tied together and rammed through the snow laying above it. The window, now covered by the snow, minimised the draft from the strong winds.

Nayati returned from his clearing duties and announced the wind and snow had ceased. Niyol suggested they go outside to get some exercise. Doli went into the storeroom and returned carrying some peculiar-looking objects that caught Yiska's attention.

Doli showed Yiska what she had collected. They were snowshoes with a difference. Made from many pieces of shaped, stout wood, tied carefully together, the shoes were as strong as and performed as well as, conventional snowshoes. Attached to the top of them were, what looked like, giant fur boots. The soles and heels moulded together from layers of leather, to a depth of about an inch and were completely flat.

Fur-lined skins attached to these, cut and shaped into the traditional boot shape. Doli put a pair on her feet and indicated to Yiska to do the same. Niyol and Yiska did likewise. They each put on their over-blankets and went outside.

At first, Yiska found walking in the shoes difficult, but soon became accustomed to lifting his feet higher than usual. They headed into the forest, enjoying the exercise the snow had deprived them of for the past two weeks. The snow was deep in the forest now, and it forced the branches on the trees down at strange angles under the weight. Each of them enjoyed the reprieve from the adverse conditions but each knew it was only temporary.

The long winter months passed at a sedate pace. Life at the cave continued, with long periods of confinement caused by the severe weather and occasional trips out for exercise, when there was a break in the conditions.

Chapter 30:
The Past

The spring thaw gathered momentum just as they were getting low on food, and it was not long before Niyol suggested a fishing trip, before the melt swelled the river to a point where their traps would be inadequate in its greater depths. Already Niyol had suspicions they were a little too late, so they tracked and hunted other prey too.

Yiska was looking forward to the trip as he had missed out on the previous hunt. As they set out, both he and Nayati noticed the eagle above them, having seen it rarely during the long winter months.

The snow, that still lay deep at the dwelling, dwindled as they descended the mountain and it was not long before it disappeared completely, except for mounds surrounding the base of trees. Nayati and Doli soon fell behind, setting snares for rabbits and ground squirrels, whilst Niyol and Yiska led Friend down the track.

Niyol turned to Yiska and broke the silence.

"It is many days since we have talked alone, and I miss this."

"You're right Teacher. I've missed the conversations and the stories," Yiska replied.

"You are content in your life with us?" asked Niyol.

"I am, but the questions in my head still will not allow me to find peace," Yiska told him.

"This, I understand. It is a problem that would cause many to leave and seek answers. The spirits have not released memories for a while. Your suffering is the reason I am thinking."

Yiska paused before answering. "The suffering is worth it, Niyol. Each time memories return to me, I find another piece of me, I get to know a little of my past."

"There is a way to enter the spirit world to seek answers, Yiska, but it is not without risk, for the spirits may keep you," Niyol told him.

Yiska looked at him with interest. "Tell me more," he demanded.

"There is an ancient ceremony I watched my father take part in. It was many years ago, and I was young. Roots of a special plant are ground to a paste; I know it still. If you eat them, they may reveal the spirits to you. If you eat too much, we will lose you to the spirits, too little and you will not visit them. When you return from the spirits, there is sickness and then it is gone. If you wish to try this, I will help, but it requires much thought before making this choice. If you find answers, you may not like what they tell you."

"I'll consider it," Yiska told him.

They fell silent enjoying the wild sounds of the forest before Yiska looked at the old man, opening his mouth to speak. Before he could say anything, Niyol, whose attention was on the trail they travelled, spoke out.

"You wish to understand what is not about you?"

Yiska nodded, hesitating before speaking. "Why do you live as you do and why must it remain a secret from others?"

Niyol regarded him for a moment, and nodded as if deciding, before answering.

"There is risk in what I say next. I am knowing you would do nothing to harm my family, but to keep the secret, to protect us all, is sometimes difficult. It is something we must all share."

Yiska looked at him, locking the penetrating gaze of his eyes with Niyol's.

"You've already brought me back from the spirits and given me a home and a family. No man could give more to another. I would do anything to protect this."

Niyol smiled at him. "This I know," he said.

Niyol told Yiska he used to work for a living on a large farm where he lived with his wife in the western manner. Life is hard on the reservation and to find new experiences and explore life away meant travel. He was content to tend the crops, his wife looked after the needs of the owners.

Their daughter had been born on the farm and she had grown up there, before she met and married the cousin of the farmer's son. The man had been gentle and kind, just as Niyol's daughter was, and everybody agreed they were a perfect match. Niyol liked the man who captured his daughter's heart and did not protest when they moved away to town to start a new life. They kept in touch over the next few years and Niyol stayed with them for long periods before his wife died in her sleep.

Devastated, the old man left, unable to stay in a place that reminded him constantly of his wife. For the next few years, Niyol returned to the traditional Navajo lifestyle, living off the land in the mountains, unaware World War Two raged across Europe and that American's had gone to fight. He discovered the cave, now his home, and lived there for some time, trying to live with his loss, until he was ready to return to the world where his daughter lived.

Yiska listened, noticing both joy and misery in Niyol's voice as he relived the episodes from his past, and the misting in his eyes. He moved closer to the old man, trying to bring some comfort.

"These memories are painful," he offered, in a quiet voice.

"This is true, Yiska, but the path you travel in the past, forms the trail of the future. If you visit the past, you see the journey from then to now, understand what is good. This is why you seek your own past."

Continuing, he told how he travelled to seek his daughter and her husband, to discover he was grandfather to three-year-old twins.

They were a gift from the spirits to replace the life force taken from him.

He stayed with his daughter and son-in-law, watching the children grow and helping in any way he could, and this allowed him to come to terms with his grief.

Then just before their fifth birthday, a hit-and-run car accident killed their parents. He did not dwell on the details but explained he had taken on the role of a parent, staying at his daughter's house and honouring the lifestyle his daughter had given to her children.

A season passed and there came a knock at the door. A man in a suit told him that because the insurance from the mortgage was not enough to pay it off, they would repossess the house. When he looked for another place to live, it brought attention to him. With little money, no job and no home he could not care for the children to suit the laws of the western people. Knowing he would lose them, he took them, before somebody else did.

He slipped away one night with the children, just a week before he was due in court to state his case. It was during June 1951.

"If I had lost them, after losing my wife and daughter, there would have been no point in living; I would have dishonoured them."

He explained the journey to the cave with two small children; hiding by day and travelling by night to ensure their safety and deciding to keep them in secret until they became adults, so no one would ever take them away. If he succeeded at this, they could follow their own journeys in life, rather than the journeys imposed on them by others.

Explaining that it was safe for them to travel with him to trade now, as they no longer resembled the children from ten years ago, still they must do nothing to attract attention and risk their anonymity. At last he fell into silence, and Yiska considered everything Niyol had just trusted him with.

"You've had a hard life in lots of different ways Niyol and yet you've achieved so much. How on earth you've survived for so long without being discovered is beyond me? Nayati and Doli are lucky to have you in their life and so am I. I'm glad you've trusted me with this, and I want you to believe I'd never betray your trust. I respect each of you, and the way you live. You're all family to me and this life is what I choose for now. One day I will leave, to get the answers I need about my past and it will be a sad day, but I give you my word I will never reveal what you've told me, to anyone."

It was rare for Yiska to say so much without pause but Niyol knew with certainty that what he had revealed was in safe hands.

"It will be a sad time when you leave, Yiska. I fear the law of the land will affect you as it would Nayati and Doli. You risk this, if they find you. They may place you in a room like the one in your memories. You will not be free. You must stay with us until you become a man, for it is my thought you are of the same age as Nayati and Doli. They will search the place you lived and will search all places for a long time."

"I have watched you these past months, and you have many gifts. You are as caring and gentle as Doli, there is also great strength. You listen well and learn; you do not use words unless needed. Already, you are becoming one with the ways of the Navajo and your skills will become as good as Nayati's."

"If you stay until you are of age, I will make you a promise."

He paused, allowing Yiska time to consider what he'd said.

Yiska prompted Niyol to continue. "What is it you want to promise me?"

"If you stay, you are no longer a guest in my home, for I see you now as I do my grandson."

Yiska stopped walking as moisture stung his eyes as the impact of Niyol's words hit home. He clasped the old man's hands.

"The spirits chose well for you to discover me in the desert and they chose well for the teaching you give me. They know you are more than just this to me," he said, pausing before adding, "Old Man!"

Niyol smiled his satisfaction. "It is settled," he said, and walked once again. Yiska fell into step with him.

A few minutes later, Doli's voice carried to them and they stopped to wait for her. She appeared with her customary smile, with Nayati following behind her, and greeted them both.

"You chatter as the bluebird they named you after," Niyol chided her.

"It is a fitting name then, Old Man!" she responded quickly.

"The traps are set Nayati?" Niyol enquired.

"They are in places that will catch," replied Nayati confidently.

"Good! Let us continue to the river."

"I fear the river will be too high and swift for our traps, Grandfather," said Nayati.

"It may be so; and then we will use the spears. There are places where the waters stay calm, we should be able to fish," Niyol said.

"I remember such places," Nayati said "Hunting with spears is good."

"It is time to show Yiska how to fish this way," Niyol said, a sudden grin broadening on his wizened face.

"This I wish to see," replied Nayati, returning the grin.

Yiska, listening to the exchange, realising they were expecting him to be the source of some amusement to them. He grinned. It seemed right; after all he was family now.

Chapter 31:
Fishing

Although they'd travelled at a leisurely pace, they made good time and were soon within a mile of the river. Journeying in silence for the past half hour, they enjoyed being outside after the long confinement the winter conditions imposed on them.

Suddenly, Doli walking just ahead, raised her hand to the others in the universal stop sign.

"What is it granddaughter?" Niyol whispered, immediately alert.

"Do you smell it?" she asked.

Each of them raised their heads offering their noses into the gentle breeze that blew towards them. Yiska and Nayati shook their heads silently, but Niyol nodded.

"Smoke!" he said. "All is damp from winter snows; it is a campfire."

"The year is young, Grandfather; we have seen none as early before," Nayati stated.

"This is true, Nayati, but many things may bring people to the forest," reasoned Niyol. "We cannot go further, there is too much risk."

"Nayati and Doli, you must see who is here, and what it is they seek. You must travel silent, in the way I have taught you, and watch from a distance. They must not see you! Yiska and I will take Friend back a way, where we will wait for your return. Go now, before the light fades," Niyol instructed.

Nayati and Doli disappeared into the trees ahead. After they had gone, Niyol turned Friend around and led him back the way they had come.

Yiska moved alongside Niyol. "Will they be safe?" he asked. Niyol nodded.

"Yes," he said with certainty. "For hunting they are skilled at moving in silence, it is necessary to get close without being seen. There will be no risk."

After travelling back for a mile, Niyol stopped.

"We will wait. Take the litter from Friend Yiska, and we will rest. We will not light a fire," he said.

Yiska nodded and did as instructed.

Nayati and Doli approached within twenty yards of a small campsite at the side of the river. The pair lay down behind a bush, thick enough to conceal them, but not so dense that they could not see through and beyond it.

Two men sat beside a fire, eating and wearing khaki-coloured uniforms with writing on the sleeves of their thick jackets. Both of them had seen this uniform before, on others, and knew they were National Park Rangers. They watched them with infinite patience for an hour, motionless, despite the discomfort of such stillness, whilst the men ate and talked.

With the light starting to fade, the men rose from their positions. One reached into his rucksack lying beside them on the ground and took out some glass containers. He passed them to his companion who produced a pen and wrote on the labels stuck on the exterior. Then they walked to the river's edge, just a few yards away, and filled them from the fast-flowing water. They screwed the lids back on to seal the contents and took them back to the campsite. There they wrapped them carefully in padding and placed them inside a rucksack. Next, they put out the campfire with earth, covering all trace of it, before putting on their packs, turning away from their unseen observers and heading down the trail.

Nayati and Doli waited for a few minutes before rising and following from a safe distance. The trail headed away from the river and widened after a few minutes' walk. The trees were thinning out, but the thick bushes were enough to conceal them.

As the men ahead did not deter from the trail, Nayati didn't need to track their footprints, they followed at a distance but soon heard voices close ahead and stopped immediately. Nayati gave Doli the signal to wait whilst he edged forward on his stomach. He spotted the men just ahead, standing behind a truck. They were discussing something as they loaded their packs into it. Entering, they started the engine, turned the vehicle and drove away. Nayati watched until the vehicle disappeared from view, before returning to Doli. After explaining what he'd seen, they started back up the trail to find Yiska and Niyol.

Darkness fell as Nayati and Doli returned to the others. After telling them what they had seen, Niyol stated his intentions.

"I think these men have left for now but may return tomorrow. They have collected water for testing, but this is of no concern to us. It is not known if they have finished. We will hunt tomorrow, but we must be careful where we go. Let us leave this trail and travel through the forest upriver, where these men will not go, for they travel by road. It will be safe for us to hunt and we will cover all traces when we leave. Now, we will make a fire and eat warm food before we sleep, for it will be cold tonight."

In the morning they broke camp and left the trail. The going was slow and difficult, as the route they chose meandered around trees and shrubs to accommodate Friend and the litter.

They heard the river long before they saw it and a tingle of excitement ran through each of them. They set up camp close to it for convenience, releasing Friend from the burden of the litter and preparing the equipment they needed for the hunt.

Swollen by recent meltwater, the river was deep and running fast; they couldn't use the traps, and the spears were the only way they could fish. They needed pools connected to, but protected from, the natural flow of the river. Niyol pointed out a pool on the opposite bank. There was a natural recess in the rock that extended for about five yards. Here, the water was still and clear, unlike the main river which was a turbulent froth of white water.

"A pool as this, but on our side of the river," Niyol told Yiska. "The water runs too deep and fast to cross," he added.

They continued upstream until Nayati grinned in delight as he spotted the pool they sought.

Each of them peered into the water. It was deep, but they could see the uneven bottom and a shoal of sizable fish. Nayati and Niyol attached lengths of sinew cord to their spears and took up a position, kneeling at the water's edge.

Because of the depth of water, they could not throw their spears; the deep water would dissipate the power of the throw as the spears travelled through it. Instead, their technique was to lower the spear into the water without frightening the fish away. They lowered them carefully until they were in position a few inches from the fish. Although Yiska was not fishing himself, his own excitement built as they lowered the spears.

"Ready," said Niyol and Nayati echoed his word.

Neither moved nor broke their intense concentration.

Nayati spoke again. "At my command, Old Man," he said, a grin breaking across his face. "Now!"

Both moved with incredible speed, thrusting down with their spears until they reached the bottom of the pool. The spears kicked and bucked viciously, Niyol's was wrenched from his grip. Nayati retrieved his, laughing in delight at the sizeable trout that flapped on the end. Doli took it off the spear and dispatched the fish with a single blow to the head from a stone. Niyol used his cordage to pull in his spear. The fish on the end was almost twice the size of Nayati's. Doli dispatched the fish.

"It would seem you have learned little, Nayati, for your fish is not worthy of keeping!" Niyol teased.

"This will change, Old Man!" said Nayati, rising to the challenge.

The fishing continued for an hour, with neither catching a fish bigger than Niyol's first. Doli and Yiska cleaned and gutted them, covered the fillets in salt and bagged them.

Niyol called Nayati and Yiska to him.

"It is time for Yiska to learn to fish," he told Nayati. "Teach him!"

Yiska assessed the weight of the spear in his hand; it was comfortable. He had observed the technique and copied it carefully as he lowered his spear into the water. He positioned it above a fish, without spooking it, and waited for Nayati's instructions.

On the count of three, both thrust their spears towards the bottom. Nayati pulled his up to produce yet another fish; Yiska's came up without. The others laughed.

Again, and again Yiska tried, but each time he retrieved his spear it was empty. He persisted, refusing to give up, but to no avail.

After half an hour of trying, he turned to Niyol and said, "While I am always pleased to amuse you all, it would be helpful to know what I am doing wrong!"

Niyol explained that the fish were not where the eye perceived them to be, due to the refraction of light in water.

To show this, Niyol dropped a small stone into the edge of the pool and told Yiska to pick it out. At the first attempt, Yiska missed the stone by a few inches before succeeding on his second. He nodded in understanding and reached for the spear once more.

He tried again whilst the others watched. The first attempt failed, to the continued amusement of them all.

On his second attempt, the kick of a fish announced its impalement, and he knew at last he had succeeded. He shook his head at the others, as he slowly retrieved his spear; they laughed at the apparent dismay on his face until he produced the fish, then clapped him with pleasure.

"I suppose you can do this too, Doli?" he enquired.

Doli nodded and took the spear from him. Yiska shook his head, in disbelief, as she too caught a fish at the first attempt.

It was still early, so Niyol suggested that they explore the river further as they didn't know this stretch of water. As they walked upstream, the river increased in ferocity so that the sound prevented any conversation. The ground underfoot became more treacherous too; larger slippery rocks lined the river. Niyol led them away from the edge to avoid them.

High above, Niyol spotted the eagle completing yet another of its orbital journeys. Accustomed to seeing it, he smiled gratefully for the sense of well-being it gave him. Always, he felt secure knowing that it guarded them all.

He observed their surroundings as they travelled, adding pictorial images to the multitude stored in his mind. The images formed maps that he could use whenever he needed. Despite the similarities to other parts of the mountains, he saw subtle features that differentiated this place, such as the peculiar shape of a tree, an unusual-shaped rock or a twist in the river. He observed all these details as they explored.

Chapter 32:
The Accident

Up ahead Nayati spotted a large tree fallen across the river, forming a natural bridge wide enough for them to cross. As they approached, he looked at Niyol seeking his approval for crossing. The tree, secured between rocks on both sides, was safe to cross and the old man nodded. Nayati led with Doli, Yiska and Niyol following.

The eagle suddenly cried out and Niyol and Yiska looked up. Niyol shouted for Nayati to stop but Nayati was already stepping out onto the thick trunk. The noise from the water, where he stood, was so loud that he couldn't hear the warning.

As he took another step forward, he cried out in sudden pain, lost his balance and plunged toward the water. Doli screamed and shot out her hand to help her brother. She caught his tunic which she held and gripped tightly, but his weight was too much for her and she followed him into the icy cold water, and the current swept them away.

Yiska reacted without thinking. Still on the bank he had not yet ventured onto the tree trunk. For a split second he watched the two of them fall into the water, before turning and running downriver. Leaving the water's edge, he found flatter ground and ran like the wind. He overtook the two bodies within seconds and changed his direction towards the water once more. Ahead a rock, jutted out into the water, and flung himself forward onto it, lying face down with his upper torso extended out over the water.

As the two of them passed, Doli was closer to him than Nayati, so he reached out and grabbed her arm, gripping like a vice. Despite his best effort though, the force of the water was too great to allow him to lift her from its clutch. Instead, he held on and pulled her sideways to the river's edge.

Suddenly, another arm appeared alongside, and gripped on to Doli's tunic. Niyol had caught up and together the two of them pulled Doli ashore. She was gasping for air and shivering violently from the cold.

"Take care of her!" Yiska shouted and once more ran down river.

As he ran, he scanned the river ahead looking for Nayati. He spotted another fallen tree that reached out halfway across the river and saw Nayati hanging on to it by his fingertips.

The tree looked too precarious to bear him so, without breaking his stride, he leapt into the water.

Intense cold shot through his body like a knife, and he gasped at the pain. He clutched at the branches and worked his way along towards Nayati who was already losing his hold as the cold numbed his fingers.

Yiska reached out, grasping his wrist just as it disappeared under the water. Nayati's white, stricken face slipped under the surface of the water but Yiska held on with all his might. Nayati surfaced, gasping for breath but was losing the battle against the cold. Yiska raised Nayati's arm allowing him to find a grip among the branches above him, but he was now so weak that he couldn't hold on.

He then grabbed the front of Nayati's tunic, turning him around to face him.

"Make your way around me," Yiska shouted at him.

Nayati nodded and, with a strength that contradicted his weakened state, edged his way towards the bank, holding on to Yiska's shoulders.

Yiska gasped as he took on Nayati's full weight as well as the force of the raging water and gripped the branch he was holding tighter. But Nayati's grip failed him and once again he disappeared under the water.

Yiska grabbed him again, this time catching his arm. He pulled it towards a branch, nearer the riverbank and held on with all his remaining strength, but he was now weakening too, and the buffeting current dragged him below the surface, almost underneath the fallen tree. His lungs burned as he tried to kick his way up to reach air.

The pressure suddenly eased but he couldn't understand why, but he still held Nayati's arm in his grip. Nayati seemed lighter, but still he refused to let go even as his body forced him to breathe. He became aware of pain as water filled his lungs just before he lost consciousness.

Niyol had taken Doli back to where Friend waited for them. It was closer than he expected, such was the speed they had travelled. He'd removed her buckskin top clothes after they had left the water and forced her to run alongside him.

Whilst it was painful as sensation returned to her body, she was otherwise unhurt, but still shivered violently as Niyol rubbed her down with a blanket and wrapped her in it. He commanded her to run on the spot and not stop until she had sufficient sensations in her hands and fingers capable of lighting a fire.

Then he left her and ran downstream again. Soon he spotted the two boys in the water ahead. He carefully crawled along the base of the tree, reached down into the raging water, grasped the back of Nayati's tunic, and pulled.

Nayati's frightened eyes widened in disbelief as the top part of his body left the water and rested onto the tree trunk, where he lay panting heavily.

Niyol clambered over Nayati and reached out his hand again for Yiska, whose eyes had closed as his head submerged once more.

Doli had disobeyed Niyol's instructions and followed behind him, surprised at the speed at which he ran. She watched him crawl along the trunk to reach the two boys, just as Yiska disappeared under the water. Fear shot through her body prompting her to action. She did not hesitate and worked her way along the trunk.

"I am here, Grandfather," she shouted, above the noise of the water.

Nayati slowly raised himself onto his elbows and edged his way back along the tree helped by Doli who took some of his weight under his arms.

Niyol still holding on to Yiska's arm, heaved, finding reserves of strength that he'd thought long gone, and raised him high enough for his head to clear the water and pull him back towards shore, where Doli was waiting to help drag him from the water.

He turned Yiska over onto his back and applied sharp pressure to his middle. On the third attempt Yiska coughed and water flowed from his mouth; his chest rose and fell but he did not open his eyes. They lumbered back to their campsite carrying Yiska between them.

Once there, Niyol took off Yiska's tunic and trousers, and wrapped him in a blanket, rubbing his limbs to restore circulation to his deathly white body.

Meanwhile, Doli helped Nayati out of his outer clothes and rubbed him hard with a blanket. She ordered him to run on the spot, as Niyol had told her, before turning her attention to starting a fire.

As the feeling returned to his feet, Nayati became aware of a sharp pain in one foot and looked down to see that it was bleeding. He remembered the pain that had made him lose balance on the tree and inspected it. A huge splinter had penetrated his moccasin and had passed through deep into his foot. It had broken off at the surface of his foot, and he could see the end of it just protruding. As splinters go, it was huge. It would be problematic to remove, and the risk of infection was present; he said nothing.

Doli spotted the wound in his foot and examined it.

"The splinter is large and is not straight," she announced. "I will have to cut round the wound to take it out."

"Do it now, my foot is still cold, and the pain will be less."

Doli nodded and set to work. He said nothing whilst she worked until she held up the offending splinter.

"I thank you for more than the splinter," he said, pulling her towards him and hugging her fiercely. "No man has a finer sister."

Doli blushed as she bound his wound. Then she warmed some water by the fire to make a hot drink. She turned to Niyol.

"You tire Old Man?" she asked.

He nodded his reply.

214

"Your strength was like that of a young man," she told him, pride clear in her voice.

She made them all tea and then turned her attention back to Yiska. His body was icy to the touch, and she looked at Niyol.

"He is too cold; he cannot move as we did," she told him.

Niyol came over to examine him for himself.

"I think this also. We need to warm him. Nayati, Doli lie next to him, share your heat with him."

As they lay down, one on either side of him, he laid an extra blanket over the three.

"Rest well, my children. And thank the spirits, as well as Yiska, for your rescue today."

Niyol sat opposite the three teenagers, on the other side of the fire, where he appeared to be gazing into the warmth of the flames. *I almost lost them, he thought, looking at them, and his eyes moistened at the relief coursing through his body.*

Later, Doli cooked some fish they'd caught earlier, and they were better for the food. Niyol told them that they would not travel home until the following day, allowing Yiska time to regain consciousness, concerned that the boy remained, once more, with the spirits. Always the spirits sought to protect him.

As he thought of the trust he'd invested in the boy, when he shared their past with him, he knew that the way Yiska acted today had vindicated every ounce of it. There was no doubt he'd saved Doli's life, but the way he'd fought to save Nayati's was incredible.

How is it that this boy becomes part of my family with such ease? he wondered.

They travelled home the next day with Yiska strapped to the litter once again. Nayati and Doli ran ahead to check their traps, but despite the number they'd set, they'd only caught three rabbits and their results disappointed them.

Niyol caught them up, just as they finished collecting the last one. Soon they rounded the rocky outcrop that signalled the boundary of their home. Nayati and Niyol carried Yiska into the cave, whilst Doli made a fire in the hearth.

Their things stored away, they sat around the fire drinking a tea that Doli had made. There was a subdued atmosphere in the cave as Yiska lay motionless by the fire.

Chapter 33:
Left to Die

The boy was in the large room putting his box away in the drawer. He locked it and placed the key around his neck. Laying back, a voice spoke suddenly from the far end of the room.

"I want that box and all the things inside it."

A silhouette of somebody with a familiar voice approached him, blocking the sunlight that poured in through the window. He shook with dread and fear.

"You can't have it; it's mine, not yours!" he replied, in a voice he hoped did not sound afraid, as the shape loomed ever closer towards him.

The profile materialised into that of a youth about six feet tall and eighteen years old. He had a scar underneath his lower lip that stretched down and under his broad chin. His eyes were small and cold, menacing in their stare and a nose flattened from multiple breaks in the past.

Two more figures appeared behind him, shorter, but just as menacing, giggling in rapturous anticipation at the intimidation they were imposing. The boy drew his knees up under his chin, inching away towards the headboard of the bed, knowing what was going to happen.

"I want that box and all the things inside it," the youth repeated, "I want it now."

This time the boy said nothing.

"If you make this difficult, you'll experience more pain than you've ever had before," he said with a malicious smile on his face.

Again, the boy said nothing.

"So be it," the youth said and shot out his clenched fist straight into the boy's face.

He cried out in pain as his lip split and his nose bled.

"Give me the key now," he said, raising his fist once more in a threat.

"No, it's mine!" answered the boy, burying his face into his hands, to protect himself from the next inevitable blow.

The assailant changed tack. "Hold him," he ordered his two companions.

They wrenched his arms from his face and pinned to the bed and his legs suffered the same fate. A rough hand ripped open his shirt and wrenched the key from his neck. The string bit into his flesh before it gave way.

Unlocked, the drawer opened, and the box removed; the boy could only watch in despair. The anger inside him built, and he struggled like a possessed demon, but was not strong enough to free himself.

"It's my box now and the things inside are mine, too. You will tell nobody about this. Understand?"

The boy remained silent, and a fist smashed into his face. Then his arms and legs were free, and he heard fading laughter as his assailants left.

The boy rose from the bed, rage flowing through every part of his body, and followed his three attackers out of the building. He kept a discreet distance and ignored the stares of passers-by, as they stared at his battered and bleeding face. He followed them to an old truck, and watched as they climbed in, one of them starting the engine.

Crouched low, the boy reached the truck, climbed onto the tailgate, and clung on as the vehicle moved off. He risked peering over the top of the tailgate, then clambered over when he realised that some large boxes in front of the cab protected him from their view.

It was only ten minutes before they stopped, and the youths got out. Hidden, he listened to their voices as they walked away from the truck, risking a glance over the side as they moved away.

They appeared to be in the middle of nowhere. The desert stretched out ahead and the road, reaching back to the town, lay behind.

The boy watched the three of them walk towards a pile of rocks a short way off and sit down in the evening sunshine. His box, in the hands of the bully, called to him. But the sun was setting fast and it would soon be dark, so the boy waited and watched.

Darkness fell, and the boy climbed out of the truck, edging away from the group in a circular route that would take him behind them. They'd lit a small fire and were warming themselves and drinking some kind of alcoholic drink. It was clear; the alcohol was having an effect because they were becoming loud, throwing empty bottles onto the rocks and laughing as they smashed.

The boy waited and waited until all went silent. He was sure they were asleep, but still he waited; then rose and made his way towards them. As he closed in, he saw his box on the ground where they were lying sprawled out. He moved within two feet of it, wrinkling his swollen nose at the sharp smell of the alcohol. He reached out, lifted the box and drew it towards him, before straightening up and starting back the way he had come. As he turned, his foot crunched on a piece of broken glass, deafening in the night's silence. He stopped, but before he could lift his foot again, the voice, that dreadful voice, spoke again.

"So! What have we here?"

They'd awakened, and a strong hand grabbed at his arm.

"Hey guys!" the youth leered. "Guess what I've caught!"

The other two rose groggily and stood either side of the boy.

"Looks like we've caught ourselves a thief," one of them jeered.

The leader looked at the boy and said. "You followed us! But I told you the box is mine now. You got a problem with your hearing?"

The boy said nothing. The leader reached out to take the box back, but the boy held on tight. A fist once more crashed into his face and he fell to the ground; this time the attack did not stop. The other two joined in, kicking and stomping him on him. He feigned unconsciousness and lay still on the ground and the beating stopped as the attackers tired.

"I think you've killed him," one said.

"What do you mean me? We're all in this together," said the leader. "Check to see if he is breathing."

The boy held his breath as one of them placed a hand over his mouth.

"He's not breathing!" he said, standing up. "Put him in the truck! No, wait; there's a large grain sack in the back of the truck, put him in that first, I don't want blood in the truck. We'll dump him in the desert."

They placed the boy in the sack and threw him on board; his head crashed against the side of the trailer and darkness engulfed him.

Yiska woke just before daylight, aware of the blinding pain in his head, and instantly recalled the memories the spirits had returned to him.

"Drink, Yiska!" said Nayati, offering him a cup. "Do not move for I see you have much pain."

Yiska drank and lay still.

"It is early, and the others still sleep; rest a while for the pain to pass," Nayati told him.

"You're safe, Nayati! I'm glad!"

Yiska closed his eyes again but could not sleep. But even as he lay there, the pain subsided, and he thought about what had brought on the return of his memories.

As dawn broke, Doli and Niyol awoke. Doli came over to check on Yiska, but Nayati put his finger to his lips. "He rests."

Doli glanced at Niyol who smiled and said, "I was sure he would return to us."

Yiska listened to the sounds and words of the people who'd become his family. He'd become as important to them, as they had to him, and it brought him great comfort.

He lay there for about an hour, before opening his eyes and sitting up. The pain in his head had almost gone, and he looked at each of them, seeing that they were no worse for their recent adventures. They took everything in their stride. He admired their strength and the way they accepted life's challenges without complaint and smiled at each of them before standing.

Although a little unsteady, he walked outside, where the air was still and clean. Snow remained present around him, thinner now, melting fast. He approached the cliff edge and took in the panoramic view; how he used to love to gaze out and imagine that all of it was his home. It was his home now, and he felt it. There was little snow left down below and he looked forward to exploring the terrain again during the springtime. Sat on a rock, he continued to stare out.

After a while, Nayati came and sat beside him.

"What you did took great courage," he started. "I owe you my life, Doli also. The debt weighs heavy, for I have not treated you the way I should."

"You do not owe me anything, Nayati, for you have all saved my life already. You gave me a home, and despite the teasing you sometimes give me, I know you didn't mean it. In fact, I take it as a challenge and this helps me to learn what you teach, faster," Yiska replied.

Nayati looked relieved, "This is true; perhaps we may help each other. But this day, you are no longer Yiska of the Navajo." He paused before continuing. "For now, you are Yiska, my brother." He placed a hand on Yiska's shoulder and added. "If it pleases you to be my brother?"

Yiska looked at him before replying, "We live in the same cave, we hunt together, and we share the eagle spirit. I can't think of anyone I would rather have as a brother; but I place a condition on this."

"Tell me what it is, and I will do it. What is it you need?" Nayati demanded.

"You must continue to be the Nayati I know, but a warning, I may return the teasing," Yiska said, laughing at the confusion on Nayati's face.

As Nayati understood what Yiska meant, he suddenly grinned and said, "It will be as you ask, my brother."

Nayati gripped his Yiska's forearms in his hands.

"I see you Yiska of the Navajo, I see the man who arrived a boy, I witness the courage you face the world with, and I see the honour you give to me, my sister and grandfather. Your ways are not all Navajo, and this is not needed for you are of mixed spirits. You are better for being strong in both ways and it is my choice to learn your ways so I can be more as you. I seek to be worthy of my brother as he is worthy to be mine."

Nayati seldom said so much in one speech and the arrival of Doli and Niyol witnessed it; Doli sat next to Yiska and kissed him gently on the lips for all to see. She turned to her brother.

"My brother now sees with both his eyes and it is good. It is a good day because of this, and it is a good day for we are all here together. The sun shines, there are no clouds and the spirits are at peace!"

She slipped her hand onto Yiska's knee and he placed his on top and squeezed it. He let it lie there, enjoying the closeness of her. She lay her other hand on her brothers and he gripped hers with his own.

Niyol spoke with feeling. "My little Bluebird is as good with words as her mother and grandmother were before her." He smiled at her. "I agree with your choice of words. We will walk in the forest, for the pleasure it gives. It will be so that we take food and travel up the mountain; it has been many moons since I journeyed this way. You are ready for this Yiska?" he asked.

Yiska nodded smiling.

They were walking an hour later, heading upwards. There was no trail to follow, and the forest became thicker as they climbed. The canopy protected the ground below, so there was little snow there, despite the increased altitude. No sooner had it thickened than the forest ended abruptly, and they stood at the base of yet another mountain. Loose scree covered the ground rising to meet the solid mass of rock above it. The snow was thin here too, melting as it bathed in the afternoon sun.

Niyol led them around the edge of the mountain, to a small clearing by a massive drop-off, much larger than the one outside their cave. They stared out at the view below; it was incredible, stretching for miles, the true extent of their forest home shown in all its glory.

"No wonder you live here," gasped Yiska, completely awestruck.

"The spirits bless us," said Niyol.

Chapter 34:
The Decision

"While I slept, the spirits returned more memories to me," Yiska said to Niyol.

"I thought this was so; the pain when you woke was as before," Niyol replied.

"You were awake?" enquired Yiska.

Niyol nodded. "It is hard to sleep when there are matters of concern."

"At last I'm aware of what happened to me, now," Yiska informed him.

"You wish to talk of it?" asked Niyol, and Yiska nodded.

"The memories continued from last time. I've seen it all from the moment I opened the box, but still remember nothing from beforehand."

"Yiska, you do not deserve what you have experienced." She had tears in her eyes as she spoke.

"I still do not understand why it happened, which worries me. Was I a bad person too, or just a victim? There are many questions I want answers to," Yiska moaned. "What do you think Niyol?"

Niyol breathed in deeply. "The memories are powerful, I believe that the spirits protect you still, for there is still more to reveal. The pain and confusion remains. Is this not so?"

Yiska nodded his reply and then asked. "Why return these instead of pleasant ones from when I was younger?"

"I have considered this, and my thoughts are not good. Maybe what happened before is worse, and so the spirits still keep them from you," Niyol suggested.

"What is it that could be worse, Grandfather?" asked Doli, in disbelief.

"That I cannot answer. Yiska will search for the memories to answer this."

"You mean leave, Old Man, to seek the truth?" Nayati asked.

Niyol nodded. "It may be the only way," he said, sadness clear in his voice.

"You said it would not be safe for him, for he is young; they would take him if they caught him," Doli whispered.

"This is so, but not now. Yiska must wait until he is older; but in time he will leave. I have been on many journeys to seek answers. The questions would not leave my head. This happens to each of us. We do not choose this."

"You are right Teacher," Yiska breathed. "Already these questions invade my thoughts regularly, they are never far away. How is it that I'm aware of things and yet I have no knowledge of anybody teaching me. Niyol said that the important thing is the person I am becoming, not the person I was. But how can I be sure that I'm better? The confusion torments me and I'd like the answers to move forward."

Doli squeezed his shoulder. "There is no confusion of who you are, you are Yiska of the Navajo. Kind, caring, true and the bravest among us, you could

226

have been no better in the past than you are now," she said, "If you leave, you may change and become different and I would not want this."

Yiska placed his hand on hers and replied, "I will not change Doli, I am proud to be Yiska and live the way we do. That will stay the same for as long as it can."

"My thoughts are this; if you decide now what you will do, you will rest without the trouble in your mind," Niyol suggested.

Yiska gazed out over the miles of forest that stretched below them, before speaking.

"Every time I listen to your words, I learn something new or see something different. You have experience of most things and from a long life. I trust what you say, and I think you are right but making that decision is difficult."

Yiska paused from further comment and the furrow lines on his forehead deepened as he concentrated. The others noticed it and honoured the silence, each knowing that a decision was being contemplated and each fearing that Yiska might leave. The intense silence stretched on and on and Doli caught her breath when Yiska spoke.

"I will stay with you here until I am 'of age', but then I must journey from this place, my home, to find answers to my questions, unless the memories return by themselves. Without them, I will never find the peace I want."

"It will be as you say, Yiska, and we will help you on your way."

Niyol rose to his feet, with a small grimace at his protesting joints, watching as Yiska held out his hand to Doli to help her to her feet. She squeezed it and her smile of relief said more than words.

"There is a matter between us that is unsettled Yiska." Nayati said, with a gleam in his eyes.

"What's on your mind?"

"A race that did not have a winner. This will happen and you will see the dust as I fly."

Yiska laughed and Nayati couldn't resist laughing to.

"So be it, brother."

They each recognised the significance of the past few minutes and Niyol sighed with a mixture of relief and contentment.

"The next part of your journey lies somewhere out there," he said, gesturing towards the vast expanse beneath them. "But for now, our journey leads us to the summit. There is a place where eagles nest…"

C. S. Clifford has always been passionate about stories and storytelling. As a child he earned money singing at weddings in the church choir; the proceeds of which were spent in the local bookshop.

As a former primary teacher, he was inspired to start writing through the constant requests of the children he taught. He lives in Kent where, when not writing or promoting and teaching writing, he enjoys carpentry, sea and freshwater angling and exploring the history of his local countryside.